Wake Up
DEAD

Wake Up
DEAD

Christopher Bonn
JONNES

SALVO PRESS
Bend, Oregon

This is a work of fiction.
All characters and events portrayed in this novel are
fictitious and not intended to represent real people
or places.

WAKE UP DEAD

Salvo Press
P.O. Box 9095
Bend, OR 97708
www.salvopress.com

Cover Designed by Scott Schmidt

Library of Congress Catalog Card Number: 99-68308

ISBN: 0-9664520-5-4

Printed in Canada
First Edition

For my parents, who instilled a life-long thirst for knowledge

Chapter 1

Paul Fontana pulled slowly to the curb. The autumn leaves crunched under the Corvette's high performance tires. Towering elms shaded a boulevard crowded with expensive foreign cars. He checked the house number. This was the place, a row house with a growth of ivy covering its brick facade. Black wrought-iron grating barred the windows, matching the railings framing concrete steps leading to the door. The landscaping was well maintained.

This might be good, he thought. These residents don't shop with coupons. Besides, tonight he had nothing better to do than ...well, that's what he was here to find out.

He pulled the letter from the glove compartment and read it one more time.

> *Dear Mister Fontana:*
> *I would like to meet with you to discuss a*
> *business proposition. I enclose a personal*
> *check in the amount of five hundred dollars.*
> *You may consider this a retainer for your time*
> *in reading and evaluating my offer. Another*
> *five hundred dollars is yours upon our first*
> *meeting. Be assured my proposition is legal*
> *and lucrative. Please come alone to my home*
> *at five-thirty p.m. on Thursday next. Your*

*questions will be answered. It would be to
your benefit to remain silent on this matter.*

Yours most sincerely,
Mason Brooks

The address listed at the bottom directed Paul across town, not far from the university.

Paul had rushed to Mason Brooks' bank within minutes of receiving the check. To his surprise, the check was good. The letter was odd, but no hoax.

He pulled down the visor and checked his groomed black curls in the mirror. Women loved his hair.

If this Brooks guy is gay...

Paul retrieved a .38 caliber Smith & Wesson snub-nosed revolver from under his seat and slipped it into the holster on his back, beneath his sport coat. He had enemies down in Atlantic City. He'd considered the possibility of a trap, but couldn't imagine them financing or devising such an elaborate ploy to kill him. This was probably some old crank who wanted to hire him to buy drugs or fence a hot item, which on second thought didn't seem likely in this neighborhood. It was best to be prepared for anything.

He killed the motor and pocketed the key. Five hundred dollars more for going to the door? Yeah.

He rang the four-tone bell and fingered the ornately carved door. Real wood.

The door opened silently and Paul saw a shorter man in his late fifties or early sixties. His grey beard was closely trimmed. His eyes held a strange excitement.

"Ah, Mister Fontana. So good of you to come. I'm Mason Brooks. Please, do come in." He spoke with a slight British accent.

Paul didn't budge. "Your letter says I get five hundred for showing up."

"So it does, and I have a check for you in the den. Please come in." He held his arm out in a welcoming gesture. "I think you'll find what I have to say very interesting, Mister Fontana."

Paul leaned into the doorway and looked at the place. The interior was neat and richly appointed—nothing to suggest a threat. First checking behind the door, he stepped in. "Are we alone?"

"My wife is home. She may join us. I have no secrets from her. You have nothing to fear, Mister Fontana. Please." He tried to seem nonchalant, but was clearly anxious.

Paul followed him into the den and sat across from him in a plush recliner. The warmth and glow of smoldering coals in a stone fireplace made the room inviting. Several achievement plaques adorned the mantel.

"Would you like something to drink, Mister Fontana?"

"The check?"

"Ah, yes." Mason rose and retrieved a check from an antique hutch across the room. He returned and stood before Paul, clutching it. "Please hear me out before you go." He paused and then handed over the check.

Paul looked it over. It was identical to the one he'd cashed two days earlier. "All right, what's this about?"

Mason sat slowly, carefully, as if a sudden move might cause Paul to change his mind and leave. "I hardly know where to begin, Mister Fontana." He picked lint off his cardigan sweater and rubbed his beard. "Let me tell you a little about what I do. I'm a scientist, a research scientist. For the past thirty years I have devoted my life to the study of dreaming."

"As in sleep?"

"Precisely. I did my thesis on neuro-physicology at Oxford in the early sixties, with a focus on the pontain reticular."

Paul raised an eyebrow. This wasn't what he'd expected.

"That's an area of the brain, Paul. Later, after coming to the United States, I joined the university here, and have since studied nearly all aspects of the human brain as they relate to dreaming. Some would argue that I'm the world's leading expert on human dream pathology."

Paul's eyes roamed from the intense gaze of Mason Brooks to the table next to his chair. A half-dozen hardcover books stood wedged between brass bookends. The name Mason Brooks was on each spine. "You're a P-H-D?"

"My position with the university has allowed me over the years to focus my research in the area of greatest interest to me: non-REM sleep. Almost all research to date, and continuing as we speak, has focused on REM sleep—"

"That's 'Rapid Eye Movement,'" Paul said with absolutely no idea why he was here or what they were talking about. Nevertheless he felt compelled to show he'd heard the term.

"That's correct. Adults have sporadic cycles of REM sleep all night long. It's what lay people commonly refer to as 'dreaming.' The eyeballs move beneath the eyelids. An internal switch in the brain activates the processes. The cycles are typically twenty minutes in duration."

Paul was rapidly concluding that this was no drug deal or proposal for larceny. "Look, Brooks, I appreciate the science lesson, but I've got to be honest; you've made some mistake here. You've got the wrong guy. I barely passed high school chemistry. I don't even watch public television. Maybe I'll just take my check and go."

A woman had been standing in the doorway for a moment, unseen, listening. She stepped forward and spoke. "Be patient, Mister Fontana. Mason tends to lose himself in his work and forget that others may not know what he takes for granted." Then, moving gracefully to stand beside her husband, she placed her hand on his shoulder and said softly, "Mason, dear, I believe Mister Fontana will be more interested in your money than your research."

Mason nodded vigorously. "Quite."

Two items suddenly rekindled Paul's interest in this mysterious visit. Money was again the topic of discussion, and this was no ordinary woman.

Brooks formally introduced the woman as his wife, Monica

Brooks. Paul immediately felt out of place and uncomfortable. Unsure of proper etiquette, he eventually stood and awkwardly shook her hand.

Monica Brooks was everything Paul would ask for in a woman if he could order one from a catalog. He had trouble keeping his eyes off her. She was a black-haired beauty with bright red lipstick and an impossibly smooth, cream-like complexion. She was built like an Atlantic City showgirl, yet carried it with class. Her black hair shimmered as if in a shampoo commercial and set her off from the many blondes he was accustomed to dating. An expensive, low-cut evening dress, accessorized with plenty of full-carat-diamond jewelry, made her absolutely irresistible. She might as well have worn neon. She was ablaze with beauty.

She was a good thirty years younger than Mason.

Paul looked from her to Mason, who was speaking again but being ignored by both his wife and guest. The older man wasn't unattractive, but looked his age. The two seemed an unlikely pair.

Man, you must have a lot of money.

Paul looked back at Monica, who was looking at him and smiling. He flickered a smile and both looked away.

Mason was trying to sum up whatever he was saying. Paul focused on listening.

"...and the point is, though the road to riches isn't paved with grants and endowments, or a professor's salary, I've managed to finance my research program. In fact, I'm quite wealthy. Frankly, Paul, I have more money than you can imagine."

"I have a big imagination," Paul said. His comment drew another smile from Black Beauty. He felt her watching him.

"I'm able to offer you substantial compensation for your participation in my research."

Paul suddenly envisioned large needles in his arm and metal instruments breaching his rectum. "I'm no guinea pig. What exactly does this 'participation' involve?"

"It's quite simple. Your sleep would be monitored, which would involve some quite painless machine hookups, but the key is, I would require your complete cooperation for an indeterminate period, possibly months. I must know your every move, sometimes even approving them. It's imperative that you agree to cooperate in the event that you're asked to change plans."

"You've lost me. Where would my sleep be monitored?"

"Eventually I can assemble additional equipment that will allow us to monitor you at your apartment, but initially the work would be done here."

"Here?"

"Yes. I have a fully-equipped research facility upstairs. I'm able to work quite independently of the university."

"You want me to sleep here?"

"That's what it would involve, yes."

"How often?"

"Every night until we set you up at your apartment."

"You want me to move in?"

"You'd be free to carry out your daily routines as you see fit, although we would always remain in close contact, and sudden changes in your schedule may be required."

Paul laughed. "How would we stay in close contact?"

"I would provide you with a pager. Your response when summoned must be immediate. This could cause you difficulty if it occurred while you were in the middle of something important at work."

"Like when I'm about to close a big sale?"

"I don't mean to belittle, Paul, but selling cars is usually not a lifetime career. You might seriously consider terminating your present employment."

Paul stared at the old man, dumbfounded. "What the hell is this? You want me to quit my job and move in with you so you can study my dreams?"

He puzzled over something else too. He didn't recall mentioning that he was a car salesperson. How much did this guy know about him?

Monica Brooks appeared to enjoy their interaction, sitting next to her husband on the sofa. Her long, close-fitting dress was split to the knee on one side. She lifted the dress slightly to accommodate crossed legs, and some thigh showed. There were no disappointments there for Paul, either.

He stretched his peripheral vision to its limits as he watched her sit and expose leg, while still maintaining eye contact with her husband. If he could get his eyes to go different directions, he would do it now. Part of him wanted to get up and leave this weird scientist and his bizarre offer; take the money and go—but he was curious to hear more. A stronger part of him hoped this was some strange, marital sex game, an invitation to sleep with the wife and satisfy her in a way the old man could no longer do, that she'd singled him out after an exhaustive search of available men in the city.

Must be the hair.

Mason looked concerned. "I realize this seems odd and a bit drastic, but you would be forwarding science more than you can imagine, and paid well for your services."

"Brooks, I don't give a damn about science, and if you think I'm going to quit my job and move in here for a few hundred dollars, you're wrong."

Please, he thought, now tell me I get the girl.

"You're mistaken, Paul. I'm sorry if I gave the impression the amount would be so small. I would pay you two thousand dollars per week for your participation."

Any poker face Paul might have wished to wear for negotiation was now on the floor near his lower jaw. "Oh," was all he could say.

Mason brightened.

Paul recovered quickly. "Hold it. Two grand a week? That's eight grand a month. That's a bunch of money over time. How many other people are you recruiting for this? How am I supposed to know you're good for the money? This sounds like some kind of scam."

"I assure you; this is no fraud. I will pay all your expenses.

You'll have nothing out-of-pocket, and there are no other recruits. I require only you for my research."

The last remark surprised Paul. He'd thought he was one of several people perhaps randomly selected.

Monica momentarily distracted him as she rose and placed another store-bought log on the fire. He almost moaned aloud as she bent over and the back of her dress pulled tight against her buttocks. He imagined the fire's flickering reflection on her leg was his tongue.

He pulled his eyes back to Mason. "Now wait a minute. Why me? What's so important about my dreams? What are you looking for? What's with the pager and this whole research thing?"

Mason looked pained. He looked to Monica standing at the fireplace, listening.

"I think you'll need to explain this to him, Mason," she said.

Again he nodded at her advice, more reluctantly this time.

"Paul, in my letter I asked that you keep your visit here a secret. Were you able to do that?"

"Yes."

"Fine. I'll have to ask that everything I'm about to tell you be treated confidentially as well. This is imperative. It's not that I fear losing my research to anyone else, and there's surely nothing illegal or immoral about it, but if what I'm on to should get out to the press or the university, I'd be so hounded that I'd never conclude my work. I must not be distracted."

He paused as if waiting for Paul's agreement.

Paul shrugged and made big eyes. "Whom would I tell? I don't know what you're talking about yet."

"How about that drink now?"

Paul nodded.

Monica moved toward a glass liquor cabinet. "What would you like, Paul?"

Paul bit his tongue to keep 'screaming orgasm' or 'sex on the beach' from coming out. "Scotch, please."

Brooks leaned forward on the sofa and became animated.

"Early researchers believed that dreaming took place only during REM sleep. They hooked their subjects up to electroencephalographs, EEGs, for brain waves; electromyographs, EMGs, for muscle tone; and electrooculographies, EOGs, recorded eye movement. These measure what are believed to be the key responses to dreaming. Such measurements are lower during non-REM—not nonexistent, just lower.

"We've since learned that sixty percent of the time people wake during non-REM sleep, they're dreaming. Some have argued that people have only remembered an earlier REM dream in such cases. The consensus, however, is that some dreaming does take place during non-REM. My research has proven this conclusively. Yet, still today, researchers overlook non-REM sleep as medically and scientifically insignificant."

Monica pressed a drink into Paul's hand. Their fingers touched. Paul actually tingled. It had been years since a woman affected him this way.

Brooks pressed on. "Over the years, my curiosity with the enigma of non-REM grew. How can it be that in a sleep state that elicits virtually no physiological dream response, when a body is purportedly in deep sleep, dead to the world, dreams still take place? I've devoted my entire career to that question."

Paul sighed and gulped half his Scotch.

Monica fingered the ice in her drink. "Mason, some of these details can be explained later."

Brooks nodded again. "Forgive me, Mister Fontana. There's so much to relate." He paused and then began again. This time there was an excitement in his eye. "Paul, have you ever experienced deja vu?"

"Sure, that's when you remember doing something at the same time you're doing it for the first time. It's as if you've been there before, though you're sure you haven't. It's a chemical brain stimulation thing, right?"

Brooks shook his head with a knowing smile. "What if I told you that it's real. The future does exist in the present, and every night each of us witnesses it in the deep state of non-REM sleep. Deja vu is nothing more than a leak from the subconscious mind to the conscious. You suddenly feel the sensation of memory, of familiarity, because you have been there in your dreams."

"I'd say, 'In your dreams.'"

"How else can you explain clairvoyance or extrasensory perception?"

"I don't try, Brooks, but I guarantee, a few ten-dollar words aren't going to convince me we're all dreaming up the future each night." He glanced at Monica and found her clever smile unsettling. "I saw your name on those books there, so I know you don't have your head wedged too far up your ass; but you ought to step out of the lab and get a breath of fresh air once in a while. Dreaming the future? Come on."

"There's more. Not only do we dream the future, we can change it through a technique called lucid dreaming. Are you familiar with the term?"

"Sorry, I must have missed health class that day."

"Lucid dreaming is the ability to become aware that you're dreaming, without waking up, and to control the dream; decide what should happen next. Essentially, if you're aware that you're in a dream, and you know it's the future that you're dreaming, you can control events in the dream, which in turn changes the future."

"And we're really descendants of apes and aliens, too, right?"

"Yours is the reaction I expect, Paul. In fact, I knew you would react like this. You'll see the light, however. I can show you proof."

"That I'd like to see."

"Excellent. Then you agree to work with me?"

"Not so fast. The money is interesting, but is there pain involved in this, any danger, you know, infected needles or electrocution, that kind of stuff?"

"There's absolutely no pain or danger. The payments will be prompt, and I'll answer all your questions. And, although I think you'll change your mind, your belief in my research is not required. Feel free to relax and accept money from an old lunatic."

"What about a contract?"

"I'm afraid I'm not much for legalese. I've drafted no documents, nor do I have the time or desire to involve an attorney. Our association must be a gentleman's agreement." He held his hand out to shake. "Two thousand per week, indefinitely, in exchange for your dreams. Do we have a deal, Mister Fontana?"

Paul hesitated and stared at the man with outstretched hand. All he could read in his eyes was sincerity...and desperation?

He looked to Monica, who wore a cat smile. Her eyes narrowed and an eyebrow raised, almost daring him to say no. He slowly reached for Mason Brooks' hand and then gripped it firmly. "If you don't mind, I prefer to keep my job."

As the two shook, Monica caught the glint of jewelry on Paul's wrist. She slid closer to Mason and took Paul's hand. "Excuse me, but I'm a bit of a jewelry nut. May I see your bracelet?"

At first startled when she reached for him, Paul pulled back the sleeve of his sport coat, revealing his gold bracelet.

"It's beautiful," Monica said, turning his hand over several times. "What does the inscription say?" She leaned close to read it.

Paul could smell her she was so close. Her head was nearly in his lap. He wanted to run his hands through her hair. "It says: Love is a bond stronger than life itself. My eternal love, Mother."

Monica looked up at him. Her brown eyes were framed within a masterful matting of mascara and eyeliner. "Your mother must be a very special person."

"Yes, she was. She died of cancer when I was two. She had this engraved for me shortly before her death. I've added a few links to the chain over the years as my wrist grew. I've worn it my entire life."

Monica smiled warmly and released his hand.

Mason was anxious to continue his discussion with Paul. "I

agreed to answer your questions. Do you have any at this point?"

"Yes. Why me? Was I picked randomly, or do you have some reason to want me for your research?"

"Paul, had you ever seen me before today?"

"Never."

Brooks appeared puzzled by that, but not surprised. "You may have been picked randomly, but not by me."

"Who then?"

"I don't know. God, perhaps? Whoever writes fate."

"Please."

"Paul, you and I are bonded together in some way I cannot understand, but for a purpose that is becoming painfully clear. I've seen you many times before today, each time in a dream, a non-REM dream. I dreamed about you so vividly, I saw details that allowed me to track you down in real life."

"What details?"

"The license plate number on your Corvette, for one."

"The license bureau doesn't give out information to just any-body, do they?"

"Wealth has its advantages."

There was something unnerving about the thought of this old guy snooping into his life. "It could be a coincidence that a plate matches the one you saw in your dreams."

"It wasn't just the plate. Your car matches, and I saw you, clear-ly, several other times."

"Why would you dream about me?"

"That's the part that's so disconcerting. Fourteen months ago I had a faint premonition, just a hunch, a sudden unexplained feel-ing that I should hesitate at a green light before accelerating into the intersection I'd stopped at. I did, and a moment later a red Corvette sped past, running the red light, probably doing seven-ty. If I'd pulled out as I normally would at a green light, my Mercedes would have been broadsided, and I'd have been killed. As the event unfolded, the premonition metamorphosed into the most intense episode of deja vu I'd ever experienced. It was quite startling."

"What proof do you have that it was me?"

"None, that time. I barely got a look at your face. My premonition was enough to change my actions and alter fate, though."

Paul frowned and shook his head.

"I learned later," Brooks continued, "that the premonition was the result of my experimentation. I have since refined the process and have seen you in many dreams."

"What process?"

"Ten years ago I established my research facility here at home so I could conduct experiments on myself—"

"What does the university think of that?"

"Using other subjects made no sense. The research was in no way dangerous or harmful, and I couldn't trust the feedback I might get from another subject. I began by making modifications to an electrocardiograph."

Paul winced inside at the mention of another big word, but kept his expression blank. In his short time with Mason, he'd concluded that questions or apparent confusion only extended the lectures. Suddenly he was very glad he'd decided against college.

The lecture continued anyway. "I created a monitoring device substantially more sensitive and receptive to the faint EEGs typically recorded during non-REM sleep. I began recording my own sleep regularly as I tinkered with the equipment and ran various experiments. Early on, I had no specific goal in mind other than to improve our monitoring capability of non-REM sleep, and to quantify brain activity."

Paul came close to holding his hand up to halt the dissertation, but the thought of the money stopped him. This might be the price he'd have to pay.

Mason sat on the edge of the sofa, his hands and feet moving spastically. "I've always been intrigued by the notion of somehow recording our dreams for later replay. If we could watch our dreams while awake, the insight we would gain on the workings of the human mind would revolutionize the mental health industry. That would be one of many possible benefits."

Maybe if he agreed, Paul thought, *it might speed things along.* "I'd like to watch my dreams, could probably even sell a few of them."

"The technology to replay dreams on a color video screen for all to see is several decades away, I'm afraid. I did know, however, of various techniques used to improve memory retention of REM-sleep dreams, one of which is lucid dreaming, so I decided to go in that direction. If we can fully recall our dreams, we at least have improved insight into our own minds and better ability to describe dreams to a psychiatrist."

Paul surrendered and sank deeper into the chair.

"So I began finding various ways to convert my new, non-REM EEGs into stimuli for the brain. I've developed a device that converts EEGs into tones and vibrations that stimulate the aural and ocular areas of the brain, simulating the same sensations the brain felt as it emitted the EEGs in the first place. In other words, it stimulates the brain, triggering conscious recall of a previous non-REM dream."

"Sounds like bio-feedback."

"That's a good analogy, I suppose. My premonition at the intersection was the first indication that my device was working. I have since made great improvements to equipment and technique, and am now able to recall almost my entire non-REM dream activity on a daily basis."

Paul's tongue explored inside his cheek.

"I've also discovered that the brain over time can be trained to recall these dreams, that the wall separating conscious and unconscious thought is porous. With practice, the mind learns to navigate from its darkest depths to the light of consciousness. It now takes very little stimulation for me to attain total recall of the previous night's non-REM activity."

"That's great, Brooks, but what does it have to do with me?"

"Everything, for me. About a year and a half ago I began experiencing an increased frequency of deja vu episodes. The premonition was the event that caused me to suspect a relationship to my research. As my successes in the lab increased exponentially, my feelings of extrasensory perception did too.

"One morning about a month after the car incident, I had a breakthrough. I was hooked to my equipment, playing back the previous night's EEG, when I suddenly remembered a vivid dream I hadn't consciously known I'd had. When I remembered it, though, it was obviously a memory, not something new. I knew then that this was a eureka, but I didn't realize how profound until later that day.

"The dream I'd recalled was a nightmare involving a flight I was to take that day. In the dream, the plane went down and I died. I have a fear of flying, so I assumed that this fear had inspired the dream. More nervous than usual, I went to the airport that day, still determined to fly.

"One of the strongest recollections from the dream was of the person sitting in the seat next to me on the plane. That person was you, a complete stranger to me at that point. When I got to the airport and saw you waiting to board the flight, I almost had a coronary. Understandably apprehensive but still skeptical, I went as far as boarding the plane after you to see where you'd be sitting. Sure enough, you were in the seat next to mine. I got off that plane as fast as I could and canceled my travel plans."

"That sounds bizarre, to be sure," Paul said, not at all comfortable with what he was hearing, "but what you dreamed didn't happen, so you didn't dream the future."

"Precisely so. I dreamed what the future would have been if I hadn't taken steps to change it. I got off the flight, so it didn't happen."

"Did the plane go down?"

"No. I don't think it needed to since I wasn't on it."

Paul guffawed. "That's paranoid."

"The flight existed and you were there. I saw you."

"When was this and where was I going?"

"It was thirteen months ago on a flight to Atlantic City."

Paul had gone. "I fly to Atlantic City a lot. Based on how much you know about me already, I'm not surprised you know about a flight I took. This doesn't prove anything except that you're a good detective or have weird dreams, or both, but you're not dreaming the future."

"But I do. These are examples of me changing the future I'd dreamed about by taking conscious steps not in the dreams—but I've been recording and replaying my non-REM activity daily for nearly two years. I have many examples of the future playing out exactly as I dreamed it."

Paul smirked and shook his head.

"Perhaps you'll find this interesting then. REM sleep is essentially a synthesizing process for the previous day's main events. You tend to dream about the big events in your day. Dreams are the brain's way of classifying events, deciphering the complex, filing the lessons and images for later recall. Dreams help us deal with life's stresses. This is why psychiatrists rely so heavily on hypnosis and dream recall. Dreams are a personal record of how we react to the world around us.

"Consequently, about ten months ago, I set up an experiment by planning a trip to the horse track. For a week before the event, I immersed myself in the subject of parimutuel betting on horses. In this way I hoped to make my excursion to the track a 'big event' so I would be more likely to dream about it in non-REM. It worked. The night before I went to the track, I dreamed extensively about events the next day at the track. I didn't know this, of course, until I'd played back my EEGs and experienced recall. I discovered that, as REM synthesizes the past, non-REM synthesizes the future.

"Armed with the knowledge of what was to take place at the track that day, I made many successful bets. I won thousands because I'd dreamed the future and made it work for me.

"I've become a millionaire by applying my knowledge of the future to betting at the track and investing in the financial markets."

Now Paul was interested. He imagined himself in Atlantic City, armed with the knowledge of how the dice would fall and which slots were about to pay off. "Can you teach me this as part of my stay here?"

"I'm afraid there's no time for that. It's necessary to invest an enormous amount of time and energy into the subject you wish to dream about, or you'll fail. I've been so short of time myself that I've been lax at documenting my discovery. We must not be distracted from studying why you keep appearing in my dreams."

"What's the big deal with that? Maybe you've just got some latent homosexual tendencies and you're attracted to me."

"I wish it were as harmless as that. I'm afraid it's much more, though. Each of your appearances in my dreams has resulted in my death. First there was the car accident, then the plane crash. They were followed by fire, an explosion, a fall, and on and on. In my non-REM dreams I see the future. I see my death. Each time, you are there."

"But it doesn't happen."

"Right, but only because I see it coming with the help of my equipment and take steps to change it. Unfortunately, the dreams are becoming more frequent. It would appear that for whatever reason, you are the harbinger of my death."

"How do you know it's me? Maybe there's somebody else there too. Maybe it's some inanimate object or something."

Brooks gave a look of surprise, as if he'd not considered that. He looked to Monica, who cocked her head as if intrigued by the notion as well. Brooks dismissed it. "No, no. Each time I die it's a different way, in a different place, in different clothing. Sometimes we're alone together; it couldn't be anyone or anything else."

Paul continued to shake his head. "This is too weird. I can't take it seriously."

"You'd better. The common denominator in these dreams is you being present at, and sometimes causing, my death. Fifty percent of the time, you get killed too, plane crash, remember?"

Paul was paying attention now. "What do you expect to find by studying me?"

"A connection. Right now I'm on my own. My life has become a living hell. Almost weekly now I dream about my death, remember it in the morning, and then try to avoid it. It's becoming more frequent. I don't know how long I can hold it off. It seems almost inevitable. I'm tied to my machine. My life has become structured. I can't go anywhere or do anything until I hook myself up each morning and recall the day's major events. I don't yet have proof, but I'm sure this non-REM phenomenon is not unique to me. I believe we all dream the future. We must all be linked in some ubiquitous pool of time and space. We dip our toes in each night and feel the waters as we dream, but the waters are not calm. There are eddies and changing currents. Our dreams are a sextant, our actions the rudder. You and I are linked, locked together. I must study your dreams to see if there is correlation. I'm afraid, Mister Fontana, my research is no longer for the benefit of the university or the forwarding of science. I am in a race against death. That is why I have no time for outside interference or helping either one of us at the horse track."

The desperation that Paul had sensed in Mason's eyes was now obvious and...justified? And if justified desperation was a term that applied here, then mustn't it also apply to Paul? Was his life in danger as well? Could this all be true?

They remained silent, their eyes shifting from one to the other, three people trying to gauge the faith the others have in the impossible, the incomprehensible.

Paul felt a strange fear. A fear unlike anything he'd felt in years, unlike the fear of losing a sale, unlike the fear that the dice won't roll his way and he'll fall deeper in debt to men who'd as soon break his legs as hear an excuse, unlike the fear of a fight or the carnage of an automobile accident. This was something different, yet vaguely familiar. A fear he'd felt as a child. The fear of the unknown, of a dark and mysterious universe, of questions with no answer, of loneliness so deep and profound that a young boy should resort to years of make-believe conversations with his dead and barely-remembered mother to retain his sanity. Not since he'd matured to a leather-skinned independent and to the point where men stop torturing themselves with the question of the meaning of the universe had he felt such a fear.

He wasn't about to start again.

Paul broke the silence with a nervous laugh. "You believe what you want, Brooks. You've got some interesting research and a hell of a tale there, but you're not going to get me to believe that if I wake up dead tomorrow it's because I dreamed it the night before. There are only two things real in this world: sex and a winning poker hand. The rest is all somebody's—" He was going to say 'bad dream,' but cut it off realizing it didn't fit with the point he was trying to make.

He also regretted the uncouth comment about sex in the presence of the lady, Monica Brooks. When he looked at her, though, she was again smiling her odd and magnetic smile. She seemed to find him amusing, if not unattractive.

Mason, however, did not seem amused. "What of our agreement, Mister Fontana?"

"Hey, we shook on it, didn't we? My word is as good as your money. I'm not backing out. I'll just exercise my option to take money off an 'old lunatic.'"

Brooks relaxed and sat back into the sofa. He sipped his sherry and looked as though a large hurdle had been cleared.

Paul wondered if there was time to get the check cashed before the bank closed. He finished his Scotch and stood to leave. "When do we start?"

"Immediately. I need to go through a final set-up of the equipment I'll use to monitor you, so the testing cannot begin until tomorrow, but I ask that you spend the evening here. We have a guest room prepared, and I think you'll find Monica's culinary talents quite satisfactory. But I must know of your whereabouts always, and that whenever possible those whereabouts are here within my sight and control. Will that be a problem tonight?"

Paul didn't like the word 'control' unless he was using it. His sales manager at the car dealership was a control freak. His various long-term love relationships had ended over the root issue of control. At least maybe this time he'd be properly compensated for the control he gave up.

"No, but I need to at least feed my fish and throw in a load of laundry. I'm a nut about keeping my 'Vette garaged too, and I don't see one here."

"Monica will follow you home with her car, assist you with any tasks that need completing, and return you here. You can garage your car at home. We'll see that you get to work on time in the morning."

"And how long did you say this project is going to take?" Paul asked.

"Honestly, I have no idea. It may quite possibly be months before I've learned anything. You see, I'm not sure what to look for. I assure you, though, I have money enough to fund your participation for a very long period. I think it will be best if we quickly drop any formality between us. I want you to make yourself comfortable and 'at home' here with us."

Paul nodded and followed Monica to the door. The view from behind was fine. His imagination ran wild with scenarios of what 'comfortable and at home' could mean.

Chapter 2

A cold front was moving in and the sun was setting fast as Monica followed Paul on the drive across town. Only the oaks still held their leaves, and this city would look better with more of both. The ground was littered with the yellow and brown fallout from the elms and other trees. It blew across the road, collecting in gutters and doorways and hiding under hedges and park benches. In just a week, it seemed, the nostalgic odor of freshly fallen leaves gave way to musty rain-rot, and the sidewalks were stained with tannin. The boulevards were lined with bare trees, stark and forbidding. They led the way from the suburbs into downtown where a decade of overbuilding drew a skyline of half-vacant forty-story office and apartment buildings. Color and light drained off the horizon. Monica dreaded the approaching winter—slush and dirty snowbanks, frozen fingers, cabin fever, and salt on the car. More than once she had considered a move to the warmth and excitement of southern climes, but never followed through. Life was always getting in the way.

In the car ahead of her, Paul's head bobbed up frequently, checking the rearview mirror to see that he hadn't lost her. She smiled to herself, realizing he was unaware that she already knew where he lived. Feeling strangely uninhibited, she suddenly passed him with a grin and sped off at a high rate of speed, quickly losing him from sight. When he arrived at his apartment building, she casually leaned against the side of her car.

Paul looked puzzled.

"We knew where to send the letter," she said, "remember?"

Paul nodded, clicked with his mouth, and shot her with an imaginary gun constructed from thumb and index finger.

"I thought for sure your Corvette could keep up," she said.

"My judgment is better than yours, my driving record isn't."

They rode the elevator in silence to the sixth of twenty-seven floors. Paul lagged in the hall, and she could feel his eyes watching her walk. Disgusted yet flattered, she allowed her hips to swagger before stopping at the correct apartment door.

"Do you always do what Mason says?" Paul asked as he let her into his apartment.

"He's a very generous man."

"I gathered that." He tossed his keys ten feet into an empty planter, a practice-perfected ritual obviously meant to impress.

"Mason is a brilliant man on a very important quest. He needs my help, and sees that my needs are met. I have no career or pressing obligations elsewhere. I see nothing wrong with handling matters that would divert him from his work."

"Don't get defensive," Paul said, stepping into his bedroom and leaving her standing alone in the living room. A moment later he returned with a basket full of dirty clothes. "It's just that he didn't even ask if you'd drive over here with me. He just expected you to."

Monica snorted. "We discussed my participation before you arrived, Mister Fontana." Stooping, she retrieved a sock that fell out of the basket and placed it harder than necessary atop the pile in his arms. "I've been his right hand for a year now, a go-fer, if you will. It's important that he not be bothered now with the mundane details of life that the rest of us have to trudge through."

Paul exaggerated a nod and headed for the door. "I don't know what Mason had in mind, but the rule here at these apartments is, you don't leave clothes in the washer or dryer. We can't leave until this load is done."

Monica smiled politely.

"Make yourself at home," he said. "I'll be right back."

She looked over the attractive and well-furnished apartment, picking up knickknacks and studying photographs on display. What was this mood of hers? Since when did she snoop and banter with strange men? She was sitting on his bed when Paul returned from the laundry room, a floor below.

His face showed that he hadn't expected to find her there.

"You don't mind, do you?" she said. "I gave myself a tour." Her hands caressed the satin sheets.

Paul leaned against the doorjamb, watching her. "Not at all." He stared at her hard now.

She held his gaze without looking away. "You have a neat apartment."

"Does that surprise you?"

"Bachelor stereotype: the place should be awash in pizza boxes and beer cans, and the walls plastered with Playmates. I looked under the bed, expecting a mulch pile of dirty clothes. Not even a smelly sock."

"You're thorough."

"I like to know what I'm dealing with."

"I entertain a lot."

"Women, I would guess."

"That's okay, isn't it?"

She smiled and bit her tongue to keep from giggling. This is terrible, she thought. What are you doing, Monica? She rose and walked past him into the living room, where she sat on the sofa.

"Leather," she said, patting the cushions. "You shop at the better garage sales."

"Rent-to-own. It's not the cheapest way to go, but they deliver and pick up. I like to travel light when I switch apartments."

"With a Corvette and a seven-hundred-dollar-a-month apartment, you must be a very good salesperson."

"I've made 'salesman of the month' a few times, but mostly I just live above my means. A bachelor's prerogative." He sprinkled fish food into an eight-sided, thirty-gallon aquarium next to a hi-fi stack and small, color television set.

"What, no piranhas?" she asked.

Paul turned his head and looked at her with an eyebrow raised. "Sorry to disappoint you." He dropped in more food and stared into the tank. "Actually, I did have a few before. They're too expensive to feed and are more boring than people think. Now I've got snails to keep the tank clean, angel fish for cheap class, and bettas for entertainment."

"Bettas?"

"Yes, these," he pointed, "Siamese fighting fish. The males start off beautiful, with long flowing fins, but they attack each other and bite off hunks of each other's fins. Sometimes a weaker one gets whittled down so much he can't swim."

"It's a real fish-eat-fish world."

Paul turned and studied her. "I don't get it. What's with you? You're young, you're smart, you're beautiful. What are you doing with Gramps?"

"It's not so unusual. It happens."

"What, love?"

"'Gramps,' as you so crudely refer to Mason, is..."

No words came to her, and she felt her expression change. Suddenly the cold, hollow feeling that had dogged her of late enveloped her again. Turning away and in a distant voice she finished the sentence with, "remarkable."

"I'm sure he is," Paul said after a moment, "but listen, if I'm going to be living with you two for however long, just tell me one thing, are you two, like..." He improvised a hand signal of interlocking straight fingers to symbolize mating.

Uh-oh. His eyes were piercing hers. She didn't dare look away. Though she did her best to put no expression on her face, she knew there was still a hint of that goofy smile.

"Let's just say that Mason has other things on his mind now."

Without asking, Paul went to the kitchen and poured two large Scotches. He pressed one into her hand as he returned, again contacting her fingers with his own, and then sat near her on the sofa.

She was glad to hear him change subjects.

"You're obviously well-educated. Did you go to school here at the university?"

"Yes...but no, I didn't graduate, and no, I have no degree," she said, anticipating coming questions, and not happy with where he'd steered the discussion.

"I won't hold it against you. I didn't go to college at all."

"Yes, I know. You attended Washington Central High School, here in town, where you managed to graduate despite a two-point-eight average. You were suspended in your senior year for drinking at homecoming. You fancied yourself a computer genius, yet dropped out of a two-year computer sciences program at vocational school after only a year. You served in the ROTC and jumped from job-to-job for ten years before discovering your knack for sales. You've never married, and have no reported children. You don't even have a savings account, let alone an IRA. You don't smoke, drive drunk, or take drugs. You do gamble too much, ignore speed limits, and have a taste for spicy food and fast women."

She cupped her hand under his chin and gently closed his mouth for him.

"None of that interests me in the least, though," she continued. "Everyone has basic file material."

"How do you know that stuff about me?"

"Mason hired a private detective to find out about you after he managed to identify you from his dreams."

"Damn. Is he still following me?"

"No. He let him go last week. He only wanted to know your basic history and where you lived and worked. A private eye can't tell him why you keep appearing in his dreams."

Paul looked upset. "I don't like that idea. I always look over my shoulder. I've had a few bad debts and dealings with contacts in Atlantic City. I never thought I'd be that easy."

"Relax. I don't think the private investigator ever tried to get close to you. All the info came from files and databases. A few phone calls were all it required. What intrigues me, though, is what a playboy like you is doing wearing a bracelet from his mother after all these years." She took his hand and toyed with the bracelet on his wrist.

"It's not so hard to figure out. Not everybody's mother dies when he's a little kid and leaves such a special memento. It has sentimental value."

Monica leaned over and read the inscription aloud again. "Love is a bond stronger than life itself." She couldn't help smiling at that. "What a thoughtful message for a dying mother to leave a young son: to let him know she'll always be with him, even in death." She cradled his hand and forearm in her arms. "You said you've worn this your entire life?"

"Ever since I can remember." He emptied his glass and set it aside. Gradually, his free hand found its way onto her wrist, where it, too, began gently caressing. "In fact," he continued, "I've never taken it off." He looked into her eyes again.

"Never? What about when you had the chain lengthened?"

"I suppose I may have taken it off my wrist a few times, like having it enlarged, and in shop class while working the lathe, but I'd put it in my pocket or something. Let's just say it's never left my person."

"That's so sweet, a real treasure."

They looked at each other and fell silent. "Hey," he said, "we started talking about you."

"Not much there," she said.

"Oh, lady, there's a lot to you. Where are you from?"

Monica sighed. "I'm from a moneyed family out of Buffalo, New York. Father and I didn't agree on many subjects, including my choices of education and career path. I've been estranged from my family for several years now, making it on my own until I met Mason, and I don't particularly want to talk about it."

"Just like that?" Paul said, teasing.

"Just like that."

"Well then, what subject were you studying while you were in school? Can you tell me that?"

"Psychology."

Paul laughed. "I should have known."

She punched him in the shoulder and they shared a smile. Their eyes met again.

Monica dared not think about how crazy and out of control this situation had suddenly become, how fast things were progressing. What had she started here? This gorgeous man's face was only a foot away, his eyes glazed over and concentrating on her mouth. As if her lips were magnets whose polarities he could no longer resist, Paul Fontana leaned forward.

Deftly slipping the kiss, she rose from the sofa and stood over him, forcing a smile to mask her panic and embarrassment. This wasn't what she'd intended. "I'll bet your wash is ready for the dryer."

Red-faced, Paul mumbled agreement, and all but ran for the door. In the five minutes before he returned, she pounded her fist on her forehead, trying to figure out what she was doing, knowing that it had to change. Besides being just plain wrong, her foolish behavior could jeopardize all that Mason had worked for.

Looking a bit uncomfortable, Paul again sat on the sofa near her, but this time not too near. They watched the fish for a few minutes before Paul finally broke the dreadful silence.

"So, I would guess you first met Mason at the university here?"

"That's correct."

"A student of his?"

She sighed and nodded. "And please don't say a word about teacher and student relationships. I've heard all the cute comments I care to."

Paul, too, apparently wished to make no further trouble today. "So you've been as close to Mason's research as anybody—closer, I'm sure—studying under him, living with him, assisting him. What do you make of this dream stuff? Is this for real?"

She stared at nothing and thought. "It's difficult to believe, isn't it? Yes, I've been close to it. He's explained it to me. He showed it to me, and it's...still difficult. Yet I've seen the evidence. There's just no explanation for some of the things he's known. Mason is a brilliant man; there's no question about that. If anybody could do this, he could. He's about to jump ahead of Isaac Newton and Albert Einstein on the list of great scientists...or he's the most clever and manipulative schnook ever."

"So you're not entirely convinced either."

"I wouldn't say that. It's hard sometimes to reconcile what our eyes see with what our minds think is impossible. I'm not emphatic or all-faithful in the existence of his discovery, but he's used it on me. It's real. Don't make the mistake of discounting his warnings about your life being in danger. One thing here is absolute: Mason believes his life is in danger." She turned and looked Paul in the eye. "He's scared."

They sat quietly for a few more minutes.

"You said he used his discovery on you," Paul said. "What did you mean?"

"You ask too many questions." She patted his hand and stood. "Let's check those clothes and get back to the house."

Paul looked at his watch and shrugged. After retrieving his clothes from the dryer and hastily folding and putting them away, he packed an overnight bag and they returned to the house in Monica's car.

The ride home was quiet and awkward for Monica. She'd had a bad feeling about this Paul Fontana coming into their home ever since Mason first proposed it and explained his preposterous reasoning. After the catastrophe in his apartment, that feeling now grew to a painful stress headache and a sour stomach.

This whole thing was going to be a disaster. She just knew it.

Chapter 3

Mason watched from the window as Monica parked the car after picking up Paul from work. Paul stayed behind Monica from the car to the front door and very obviously ogled her backside.

Instantly, rage flashed over Mason. Seeing the impudent young man eyeing his woman stirred emotions he'd not felt for decades. With conscious effort the rage passed as quickly as it had come. The man was only exercising human nature, after all. Surely Paul wasn't the first to ogle her, or the last. Mason couldn't expect men to close their eyes every time she entered a room. In a way, he was proud to show her off and claim her as his. Besides, he'd extended the invitation to the man, and for good reason. Now was not the time to lose his temper and do something rash that might cause Paul Fontana to break their new agreement, not after all he'd gone through to get this far. Personal feelings would have to wait. He did his best to hide his anger.

"You see?" he said to Paul as they entered the house and shook off the cold, "I know when to expect you because I remember from my dream when you arrived."

Paul waved him off. "Spare me. Monica already prepped me. She said you'd know when I got here, but if she knew when to pick me up, it's a no-brainer for you to guess within a few minutes when we'd arrive home. You don't need a crystal ball for that."

"Perhaps, but Monica and I did not discuss the matter."

"So what? You could have been sitting here all day for all I know, just waiting to make your point. What are you trying to do, sell another book?"

"That's hardly my style, Mister Fontana."

"It would've been nothing to have your man find out my working hours. Your standing here means nothing. You'll have to do a lot better than this to convince me you dream the future."

Monica smiled and shook her head as if Paul were slow to catch on to something obvious to everyone else.

Paul scoffed. "Okay, fine. You two play your little game. Be condescending. For me it's better than the alternative."

"What's that?" Monica said.

"Belief."

"Did you sell many cars today?" Mason said, momentarily abandoning the subject. Paul opened his mouth to speak, but Mason immediately interrupted him.

"No! Don't tell me. You quit your job, didn't you?"

"How did you know?"

Brooks beamed proudly. "I just now remember your telling me."

"But I didn't tell you," Paul said, exasperated.

"No, but you were about to. Deja vu."

"Baloney. Deja vu lets you know something as it happens, not before."

"With a little work it lets you know beforehand. Impressive, yes?"

Paul scowled. "You called the dealership and found out."

Mason shook his head.

"I told Monica in the car. You've got it bugged."

Mason deflated. "I had hoped you'd see proof of my accomplishment for what it is. I'll need to be more patient with you, I see."

"I thought I didn't have to believe you."

"As you wish. You'll forgive me, Mister Fontana. I've invested my lifetime laboring on arguably the most important scientific discovery in the history of man. I admit I'm anxious to share the results with others, a human weakness of mine. Unfortunately, I face nonbelievers. It's frustrating. I can imagine how Copernicus must have felt."

Monica hung jackets and put away shoes as the men made their way to the den. Mason caught Paul watching her again, the lecherous eyes never letting up until she left for the kitchen to start dinner. When Paul did turn away, Mason stared him in the eye. For an awkward moment it seemed his overconfident guest didn't know what to do with his eyes, reminding Mason of a little boy caught with a girlie magazine.

Paul hastily continued their discussion. "So I suppose I don't need to tell you why I quit."

"I wish you would. My ability to recall the future is limited. The bulk of what I become aware of each morning as I review my dreams are the one or two key events of the day, and something best described as the general feel for the day. Is it going to be a good day or not? The rest of the day and all its little moments play out to what I call a heightened sense of deja vu, which also flows in waves of varying intensity. I'm often suddenly struck with a clear picture of what's about to happen even though I didn't 'see' it that morning, although most events transpire and generate recall as they happen—just as you describe deja vu. It would appear that I won't recall why you quit your job until you refresh my memory."

"How convenient. Anyway, it was no big deal. The morning wasn't going well and I've wanted to tell that sales manager there to bite it for a year now. I got to thinking about all this easy money I was going to make over here, and you wanting me to quit and all, so I said to hell with it."

"A wise decision, Paul. This will make matters much less complicated. Come, let me show you; I worked today setting up the monitoring equipment in your room. We're set to go for your first hookup tonight."

Mason led Paul across exquisite oriental rugs and hardwood floors, up the multilevel staircase and down the hall to the right to the nicely furnished bedroom he'd put Paul in the night before. Mason had spent a good portion of the day situating expensive and complicated electronic gadgetry alongside Paul's bed. The array included more than a dozen metal-sided boxes with digital screens, separate monitors, computers, printers, plotters, and a tangle of wires.

"This better not make much noise," Paul said. "I'm a light sleeper. With all this stuff in here, I may never have any dreams to analyze."

"Nothing more than a soothing hum."

"What's all this?"

Mason gave a lengthy and jargon-filled description of the setup. He could have gone on indefinitely, but Paul rolled his eyes and interrupted him.

"I'm sorry I asked," he said. "So, you think after a few nights of this contraption sucking on my brain I'll have a career writing horoscopes and fortune cookies?"

Mason was stoic.

"What part of my body plugs into this thing?"

"We simply attach several of these electrodes to various strategic locations, quite painless and harmless. Monica will take care of that for you each night. She has become quite adept at it."

"Kind of like tucking me in, huh?"

Mason glared, and Paul's sheepish grin faded fast. "Perhaps, Mister Fontana, but you're not a little boy, and she's not your mother."

Paul's relentless wisecracks were wearing thin. Mason Brooks would choose someone other than Paul Fontana to be bonded to now, if the choice were his to make. The feeling was clearly mutual.

Mason turned and led Paul to the dining room, making a concerted effort to hold his tongue for the good of the cause and wishing his annoying guest would do the same.

Chapter 4

For the third time in a half-hour, Monica appeared in the living room doorway where Paul was watching television. He didn't understand what the first two brief visits were about, and this one was just as mysterious.

He wished she would spit out whatever it was she wanted to say. After an eternity of leaning in the doorway and shifting from hip to hip, trying hard to appear as if her presence was purely spontaneous and random, Monica finally spoke.

"What are you watching?"

What inane garbage was this? Obviously she had something on her mind; anyone could see he was watching football. But other thoughts had so preoccupied him, too, he'd paid little attention to the television, and had to concentrate before answering her.

"It's the Michigan-Indiana game."

"Is it the play-offs?"

It's okay, Paul, he thought. She's a woman. You've dealt with this before. "No, this is college ball," he said, trying to remove all sarcasm from his voice.

He looked over at her from his recliner, and she nodded vaguely, staring straight into the television set. He measured her with his eyes now, continuing his earlier contemplation, trying to figure this lady out. Something about her and the old man didn't fit. He prided himself on being a showroom-floor psychologist. He could read people, understand what made them tick. It helped him sell. He could spot a sucker across the lot, then swoop down upon him and take his money without a hint of conscience.

It helped him with women too. He spotted their weaknesses, hot buttons, and desires. This helped him subtly maneuver the women into his bed.

This one, though, this Monica Brooks, smooth talker and smooth walker, was an enigma, total class and refinement, and apparent brains. How else could a Ph.D. stand her for so long? He'd have starved from lack of intelligent conversation long ago. She had handled Mason too, calmly advising him at Paul's first meeting. She was a lot more woman than Paul was accustomed to. She intrigued him and, more to the point, stimulated him.

Why are the good women always taken?

"What are you and Mason doing out there?" he said. There was so much more he really wanted to say, probing personal questions to ask, ploys to experiment with, but the debacle at the apartment the day before changed everything. That must never happen again. Now he must hold his tongue. The best way to accomplish that was to maintain his distance from both Mason and Monica.

"We're reading in the den. There's a fire going. You're welcome to join us if you wish."

Looking at her, he couldn't stop thinking that he'd like to do a little "joining" with her. Thinking might be okay. No more trying though. "I'll just catch the end of this, I think."

"Are you excited about starting your testing tonight?"

"Should I be?"

"You never know; it could be very illuminating."

"Why? I don't have to sleep with the lights on, do I?"

That earned a giggle, which caused a jiggle, and any movement she made was.... Stop torturing yourself, Fontana.

This was going to be an interesting, though trying, stay with the Brooks, he could see. Mason would study him, and he would study Monica.

What was Monica after?

Yesterday he'd seen vulnerability. There was no understanding her yet, but she was human after all, and the relationship with Mason had a chink somewhere. Another man might have backed off for the sake of decorum when she failed to defend Mason, but Paul thrived on conflict. He loved the excitement of a situation where others felt uncomfortable. That's why he loved sales. He could say or do bold things that made people uncomfortable, and he was instantly in control. That's why he'd employed his favorite tactic, the blunt question, and probed into their sex life; it was all-telling. Weak-willed people answer blunt, intensely personal questions simply to avoid conflict and embarrassing scenes, even if they don't really want to. Her answer may not have been the truth, but she didn't say "shut up, it's none of your damn business," so Paul learned a little.

Although her answer failed to tell him all he longed to know, it did reveal one important fact: this woman was deprived of intimacy. To waste such beauty was a crime nearly as bad as adultery. He knew many men who required less justification than that to chase married women.

He wasn't one of them. That's why his earlier actions both astonished and embarrassed him.

She stepped forward and bent over in front of the television to check the channel guide lying on a low coffee table, passing so close to Paul on her way that he felt her aura touch him as if it were a living thing. He raised a hand behind her as if to grab her, but slapped it down with his other.

"Is there another show you'd rather watch?" he asked. "I can leave and do something else."

She turned and smiled. "That's kind of you, but no, I'm sure this is the most important thing on right now."

That smile, the same one she had slapped him with yesterday after his lapse of judgment and restraint while he sat there blushing, had much hiding behind it.

Somewhere behind that smile she wanted him as badly as he wanted her. He could feel it.

This time, as she left the room, she closed the door behind her.

The door had been open all along. The television wasn't too loud. They certainly weren't bothering him. Why close it? Was she sending him a message? Was he doing something wrong? It felt as though all their conversations were jousting contests, but what was the prize? What was the reason? He was equally to blame, of course, and that would have to stop. Suddenly he wished he could start all over with Monica. Or better yet, had never accepted Mason's stupid proposition.

The whole notion of dreaming the future was ridiculous, but Mason's claims and the occasional impressive trick were creepy. Monica's warnings and uneasiness with Mason's purported abilities only served to further unnerve Paul.

He should have cashed that first check and never shown up here.

Now an internal debate was finally settled. At his apartment yesterday, as he'd put a few items in his overnight bag, he'd weighed the pros and cons of whether to include his pistol. The gun made him feel safe. It would do no good to leave it in the apartment, nor should he take it to work. The whole situation with the Brooks was a big unknown, too threatening to forego the protection offered by the handgun.

He had made the right decision then and was now glad he'd stashed the weapon in his room upstairs at the Brooks' home.

Chapter 5

Mason and Monica sat in the warm den reading books. A blaze in the fireplace crackled and flickered shadows across shelves of books and knickknacks set into the walls. Paul was watching college football on the television set in the other room. Mason lowered his book to his lap and stared at Monica for a time as she read, slouched with two hands holding her book in front of her face. There was no conversation between them, as had become the trend recently.

Something was wrong between them, and the chasm was widening. That was unfortunate. His research no longer left him with the time it would take to set things right between them. Maybe that was no longer possible anyway. The magic was wearing off. She no longer worshiped him, and that was a problem. Without that reverence, there was nothing but a thirty-year age gap between two people with different backgrounds and interests. Not much to base a relationship on. However, there was much to base bitterness on.

He had to try, though. "My mind has been drifting back to early in our relationship, Monica."

Her book lowered an inch, and she peered over it for a moment before raising it again to cover her face. She said nothing.

"I loved you the moment you stepped into my class, you know. You were a twenty-four-year-old goddess."

Her book didn't move, but her mouth did. "You lusted after

many coeds over the years, I'm sure."

That was true, but he'd never acted on those impulses before Monica. He couldn't have broken the taboo if he'd tried; he was just an old professor to his students, until his research began yielding results.

"You were always different from the other girls. You seemed more mature."

"Or more gullible."

She was no more gullible than most, he knew, only more vulnerable. She had few friends and held mostly to herself, cleverly and politely repulsing one young suitor after another as if holding out for something better. With her looks there was never a doubt that she could achieve her goals in life, but to her credit she didn't try to capitalize on nature's gift. "No, you were studious and always driven by a deeper fire."

"I got deep in the fire, all right."

He kept trying. "I mean that you accomplished a lot on your own, dear. You should be proud of that. You didn't have the support network others could rely on."

That was the fact that left her susceptible and fueled Mason's interest from the start. As his research and his understanding of it progressed and he began to contemplate its power over human interaction, he saw Monica as a candidate for experimentation. Inspired in part by professional interest but mostly by fantasy, he wondered in what ways his budding ability to foresee the future could affect their relationship as teacher and student.

Monica moaned.

"Did I ever tell you that I used my position with the university to access your personal file?"

"What motivated you to do that?" she asked.

"I knew you were an intelligent woman, of course, but rumor held that despite your fine academic record, you were attending the university without scholarship at higher, nonresident tuition rates. I was curious about you, wondering if there was any way I could help someone of your potential. When I discovered that you were paying your own way with student loans, personal savings, and earnings from odd jobs, and no assistance from family, well, I knew right then that I must do something for you."

"Purely philanthropic, huh?"

"Initially, yes."

"Mason, you've been a cad. Don't start lying to me too."

"Later, certainly, personal feelings entered the picture, but only after wanting to help an extraordinary student. I was very taken by your plight, what with your financial dilemma and unfortunate childhood."

He learned from Monica that she grew up under a tyrannical father who she felt had been overly critical of her every choice, including men, employment, college, and the like. She had severed all ties and was determined to prove to herself that he was wrong.

To Mason it meant little interference from meddling parents, so for the first time in twenty-four years of teaching he acted on his impulses.

"Mason, first you learned to control the future. What are you trying to do now, rewrite history?"

She was right, of course. His motives were never virtuous in dealing with her, and it was a rewrite that he hoped to sell her on. The truth was, he had carefully observed her reactions as he used his newfound abilities to astound her. Asking her to stay after class one day, he told her that her work impressed him and he would be honored if she allowed him to tutor her privately. This flattered her. Their first meetings took place at the university.

"Monica, dear, I hardly see much evil in a gratis offer of private lessons."

"During which you showered me with minor predictions about the turn of current events. Always correct, of course."

"You were impressed, as I recall."

She practically spit in her book. "That was the point, wasn't it?"

Yes it was, and he had bolstered the respect thus earned with additional flattery. Claiming she was gifted in the field, he persuaded her to make psychology her major and career choice. When he said he'd be honored to have her as a colleague in his ongoing private research, respect turned to admiration.

His uncanny ability to know her feelings, choices, and even the words she was about to say, 'because he had been at the same place earlier in his career,' helped convince her that fate had led her to her chosen career and that she could do no better than to share it with the venerable Mason Brooks.

"I wonder if you'd act differently with the circumstances reversed," he said. "It's hard not to utilize all of one's abilities in the pursuit of one's greatest dream."

"There's a difference between braggadocio and manipulation."

"A fine line."

"Like the line between innocence and malevolence?"

"I always did my utmost to remain the consummate gentleman."

That he had. They began working together after-hours at his home. They dined together. They discussed world affairs, Mason ever so prophetic. Always he was helpful and polite. Never was there a hint of his hidden intentions.

"Yes, Mason," she said with a mock British accent, "you exhibited a chivalry and charm bred at Oxford, and unmatched by any man of my acquaintance." Then, dropping the accent, she added, "Remind me never to compete with you at charades."

He wasn't getting far with the benevolence tack. Perhaps if he flavored it more with the financial aspect, it might sway her. He could help her recall how he had insisted on paying high wages for her services as research assistant, turning her admiration into adulation, and how awed she was when she first joined him for a successful day at the horse track, seeing for herself his enormous moneymaking ability.

"I don't remember your complaining when I explained that I'd personally retired all your debts and asked you to drop your classload and work with me full-time."

That didn't come out quite right. Her sarcasm had bite. He was getting defensive, quibbling. That would never work.

"Oh, no. You're absolutely right. I was hooked. When you professed your wanton and undying love for me, I was confused and in need. I decided it was love. Silly me. It's funny what a few million dollars and super powers can do to a girl."

Indeed, he thought. He kept her completely off balance for weeks, stepping up his prophesying and showering her with expensive gifts and attention. When they made love, it was at first awkward and she was surprisingly inexperienced, but a quick learner. Soon the sex was beyond Mason's expectations.

The mention of money wasn't accomplishing his goal here, but he didn't even want to touch the topic of sex.

"Perhaps we erred in moving in together so soon," he said. "After all, only fourteen weeks of tutoring and dating before living together hardly seems enough. Maybe if we'd given ourselves more time, our relationship would be stronger today."

"Yes, a lot more time."

As it was, when Monica moved in, Mason immediately took a sabbatical from the university to pursue his research and enjoy life more fully. As a widower with no children, and no siblings within five thousand miles, his pursuit of the younger woman raised few eyebrows. His absence from the university helped reduce the scandal. Monica informed her family months later of her live-in arrangement with a man they had not met, when the long delay could cause maximum pain, a way of rubbing her father's face in the fact that he was an unimportant person in her life. Mason knew from their first meetings that part of Monica's interest in him was due to the satisfaction she would get from knowing her father would disapprove. She was not disappointed.

Mason's conquest had been complete. He manipulated a beautiful young woman into loving an old man. The power he wielded then was enormous. But what about now?

"I shouldn't have to justify my actions. No one has been hurt. To the contrary, Love, you are well cared for and financially set for life. Others would consider themselves lucky to live in such an environment of learning and mental stimulation. Could you have had it better with the lawyer, doctor, screen star or investment banker you would have otherwise wed? You could have done worse."

"My hero."

There was justification for his actions, but not the kind Monica was likely to appreciate. She was his reward for a lifetime's work resulting in the greatest discovery of the millennium.

When made public, his non-REM revelations would make him as famous as Edison, Einstein, Galileo, or Da Vinci, but that wasn't what he longed for. He was satisfied to be well-known and respected in his field. As a middle-class professor and aging widower, there were less lofty pursuits now within reach: money and women. He felt little shame for vigorously pursuing what he deserved. Also there was the knowledge that his courtship of Monica, while deceitful, had been for the advancement of science. What happens to the loves and lives of Monica Westfield and Mason Brooks is of little consequence in comparison to the knowledge passed to future generations.

His reward was now in jeopardy, though, ebbing slowly, yet interminably, away. While love had actually grown between them as their first year passed, Monica's assistance in the research ultimately revealed the methods employed to win that love. That knowledge was a cancer growing on their relationship.

Mason sighed a deep, frustrated sigh. The charade was ending, and as her bitterness grew, his remorse declined. What could he do to turn the course of these opposing forces?

As Mason watched, his lovely Monica finally lowered her romance novel to her belly and took their conversation seriously.

"You can drop any pretense of Platonic love, Mason. It's pathetic."

She tucked her legs neatly under her on the leather sofa. She was the most beautiful woman he'd ever seen. That was what first attracted him, and it still had him captivated. So she had a good point. They were too different in other ways, and their relationship had started on a foundation too low to support any heavier meaning. He could probably duplicate his success with other women, but he didn't want to. He had chosen her. He was proud of what he had accomplished in ensnaring her. She was his. The thought of losing her now stirred emotions in him not felt since his teenage years.

Now there was a new, unexpected threat. A handsome, young, unattached man was living under their roof. Already he'd expressed interest in her. Paul Fontana, the man destined to take Mason's life. Was he first to torture Mason by destroying his love life? Why was this happening?

"I don't like the way he looks at you," Mason said.

Monica raised the book again. "Oh, so he finally blurts it out. That's what this is all about. You sound jealous, Mason. That's not very becoming."

"Yes, I suppose I am. It's just that he...I don't want to lose you, Monica." Nothing he said seemed to sound right.

Monica pretended to keep reading and turned a page before answering. "You've got more important things to worry about right now, dear," she said, apparently referring to his recurring premonitions of death.

Mason said no more. Despite his best efforts, their entire conversation was less than reassuring. He tried but couldn't think of a way to stop her from slipping away. His tricks no longer worked. She was right about priorities. He needed to stay focused on preventing, or postponing, his coming death. With the successful resolution of that he would at least remove the bothersome salesperson from his life.

With Fontana gone, one more threat to his shaky union with Monica would disappear as well. Then he would think of some way to keep her.

After glancing at his watch, Mason repeated his instructions to Monica on the setup of Paul's equipment, then excused himself to begin his nightly ritual dream-sleep.

Chapter 6

Monica finished reading the same page a third time and realized she still had no idea what it said. She was thinking of other matters. The conversation with Mason upset her. And how rude it was of their new guest to waste the entire evening in front of the television set watching football. He could have at least joined them for a few minutes of polite conversation after dinner.

The sudden realization that she had sat staring blankly at an open book for the past hour, secretly hoping Paul would join her for further flirtation, did not appeal to her. Nonsense. The man is a cretin, a Neanderthal. A handsome one, yes, but he misjudges the significance of that to the woman of this house.

Closing the book, she quietly climbed the stairs to tend the equipment in Paul's room. She turned on each component and carefully checked Mason's prescribed calibrations. She turned down the sheets and fluffed the pillow. Satisfied that all was in order, she paused before calling Paul for his final instructions, and surveyed the room.

His overnight bag sat neatly at the end of the bed, a pair of deck shoes beside it. The bag was empty. He was already unpacked. She opened a few drawers and checked his layout. He was definitely tidy.

Something clanked when she closed the last dresser drawer. The drawer wasn't closing fully, catching on something with a quarter-inch to go. She tried it two more times. Still it stopped short, feeling as though something heavy and solid had fallen behind it. She had thoroughly cleaned this room before Paul's arrival, dusting the dresser inside and out. Wondering what she could have dropped back there, Monica pulled the drawer all the way out and squatted down to look inside.

She gasped and almost spilled the drawer's contents. Inside the cavity, leaning against the back of the dresser, a revolver balanced on its handle and barrel over the drawer's runners. Even in the poor lighting and from the side angle she could make out the brass casings in the cylinder. This was a loaded gun.

She gazed at it in amazement for a moment, not understanding how it got there, then realized, of course, that it belonged to Paul Fontana. The pistol was intriguing. She reached in tentatively and pulled it out, handling it like an egg. Her heart raced as though someone had just thrust the weapon in her face. She turned it over in her hands, studying the terrifying object. In the dark recesses at the front of the revolving chambers, the copper-tipped, dome-ended bullets were clearly visible.

Panicky, she quickly set the gun back in its hiding spot and fumbled to replace the drawer. She had just shut it to its new, unintended stop-point and was standing awkwardly in the room staring at nothing when Paul Fontana strode noisily through the door. Startled, she jumped and let out a muffled screech that so surprised Paul, he, too, jumped back and clutched at his heart.

"Is this the right room?" he asked.

"Damn you," Monica said. "You scared me to death."

"Are you snooping on me again?" Paul said with a grin.

Monica guessed he didn't suspect what she'd found. "I was making the final preparations on the equipment. If you're finished with your football game I'll check you out on this and hook you up for the night."

"What's wrong with football?"

"I didn't say there was anything wrong with football. If you like to waste your entire evening watching grown men play a child's game, that's your prerogative."

Paul put his nose in the air, flared his nostrils, and imitated British royalty. "I say, m'lady. I cawn't imagine an evening so uproariously eventful as sitting about the library reading books for hours on end."

"It's not so bad. You should try it. I'm sure we could find a book or two with pictures for you."

Paul smirked and pointed a finger at her. "You're a clever one, you are. For your information, I had a huge wad riding on that game, and my odds increase if I'm watching."

"Superstitious too? My goodness, with your intellect you'll be tutoring Mason in no time."

Paul sat on the bed and removed his shirt. Monica couldn't help but notice that the hair on his chest closely matched the hair on his head.

She moved in and began attaching electrodes to his head and chest. As she leaned in close and touched him, it was as if electric current passed through him. With each touch she felt the energy released, tingling up her arms and coursing to parts dormant for too long. She knew without words that he felt the same.

Paul pulled the top of his pants open with his thumb and pointed inside. "You'd better put an electrode in here too. I get some pretty stimulating dreams. We'll give old Mason some stuff he hasn't seen in a long time."

Monica bit her lip hard to stop a smile. "You must remember the cause here, Mister Fontana. We're trying to save a man's life. This isn't all fun and games."

"I'll get right on that, ma'am. Is there a special position I should sleep in that will help? Or maybe I should read all the books the good doctor has written and try to get up to speed on the matter."

Monica pushed him back so his head was on the pillow. "I know it's hard for you to believe in Mason's research, but you wait and see. In a few days he'll have you convinced."

"He really believes he can see the future and I'm going to kill him?"

"Yes, and I think you're already getting to him."

"What's that supposed to mean?"

"Nothing. Now believe it or not, you can help by sleeping in a special position. Try to lie flat on your back and minimize your movements. The electrodes stay attached surprisingly well, but will come off if you're tossing and turning. Are you an active sleeper?"

"That depends on whom I'm sleeping with."

"If you're trying to impress me with your incredible wit and charm, Mister Fontana, you're failing." As the words crossed her lips her eyes ran the length of his bare torso. He was a well-built man, not overly muscular, but nicely proportioned. And the hairy chest: it started as black fuzz circling his navel and rose past his sternum and ribs in an ever-expanding plume of growth, spreading into a delicious and inviting black forest over his pectoral muscles.

Suddenly she was aware of his hand on her waist. She quickly grabbed the hand, pulling it away and holding it out in front of her.

"I hope," she said, fingering his bracelet, "that you were about to show me your mother's gift again. It's the nicest thing about you." She dropped the hand on his stomach.

Paul sighed. "I was hoping you would fluff my pillow. It's the least my mother would do for me."

"I'm afraid I'd come up short in a comparison to your mother."

"I don't know about that. You know, they say men seek to marry women who remind them of their mothers because of a secret desire to return to the womb. I think that—"

Monica interrupted. "I'll say good night now, Paul. Remember, no jostling. And don't touch the equipment." She walked to the door.

Paul leaned up on an elbow and asked as she went through the door, "Monica, you say that Mason will watch my dreams recorded here?"

"Mostly he'll have you review them and try to recall, but yes,

I'm sure that he'll review all the material as well. Why?"

"Just a thought. Wouldn't it be bizarre if I did kill him?"

The gun she had so quickly forgotten suddenly filled her mind with a terrible vision. "What do you mean?"

"Do you think his ticker could take the shock if this getup records me having a dream about his wife?"

She frowned and closed the door behind her.

Chapter 7

Monica woke to the same thought she'd had when falling asleep: Paul Fontana. Though she tried, she couldn't stop thinking about him. She punched her pillow and rolled over again.

This shouldn't be happening to her, not now, with life so complicated and her love-life crumbling. How could she be attracted to such an unsophisticated, undereducated, oversexed egomaniac?

The answer was easy yet complicated. Paul Fontana was a gorgeous man, with an excitement about him. Despite herself, she found him humorous as well. These were qualities any woman would find attractive, but they were superficial. She wanted more, a man with depth like Mason Brooks. Did Paul have depth? She didn't want to invest the time needed to find out. She'd rejected a hundred like him in the past. So why now? What had changed? Why was she finally succumbing to the wiles of a lesser man?

The answer, of course, was Mason. Their private vows and public charade of marriage were meant to prevent infidelity and protect her from men like Paul. Instead, they were now at the heart of her weakening will. There was the flattery, something she was accustomed to regularly before Mason, now reduced to an occasional lewd stare. Paul Fontana's sly and indirect compliments were surprisingly effective. She realized now how much she missed the flattery.

There was the sexual aspect. She had been young and naive when she moved in with the older Brooks. Sex wasn't a top priority for her then. After a brief flare-up, the flames of passion quickly dwindled, and their later problems were like ice water on the libido. Paul Fontana had what it took to rekindle such a fire. Mostly, though, it was knowing what her relationship was founded on that caused temptation. Mason Brooks had tricked her, used her. She was a sexual plaything, an object, a trophy. He was worse than Fontana's kind. Playboys like Paul were at least straightforward. Mason was a conniving snake. Each day the knowledge of what he'd done ate deeper into her heart. The love cooled, respect became bitterness, and adulation became loathing. Within hours of Paul Fontana's entry into her life, he became the catalyst to the end of her relationship with Mason.

So why not do something about this? Two reasons.

One answer she liked. She considered herself a lady, someone with dignity and scruples, a woman who carried out commitments without allowing their challenges to blow her into the arms of temptation like a leaf in the wind.

The second one was less virtuous, and she denied it vigorously. It was about money and need.

In any event, there were proper ways of handling this problem and, whether she chose to stay with Mason, falling into the clutches of a Paul Fontana was not one of them. She had been playful and flirtatious with Paul. The intent had been more mischievous than unfaithfulness, but she helped create this mess. It would have to stop, today.

She glanced at the clock on the nightstand. It was already after seven a.m. Mason would be finishing soon in his office. Each morning he rose at six a.m. and spent an hour in his research facility at the end of the hall—what had been the master bedroom—hooked up to what he termed his 'replay equipment,' reviewing the previous night's non-REM dream activity to see what the day had in store for him. It was fundamental during this process that he devote full attention to the replay of his dream stimuli, the sounds, vibrations, and impulses that trigger the conscious recall of non-REM dreams. Silence and atmosphere were paramount to a successful review. Her strict instructions were to never interrupt him for any event short of house fire.

Her first task that day was to inform Mason that his purported future killer had brought a gun into his house. Oddly, she felt reluctant about having to tell, as if she were tattling on a friend. It could prompt Mason to turn him out, but then that might be for the best. After all, this was a gun, a serious matter. She rose and dressed, intending to wait outside Mason's door so she could tell him first thing.

Mason barged through the bedroom door and slammed it behind him. One look and Monica knew he was irate. "Son-of-a-bitch!" he said, his accent adding an odd quality to it.

Monica immediately understood that he had foreseen her telling him about the gun. Without thinking, she jumped to Paul's defense.

"I'm sure there's no need to be so angry with him, Mason. I doubt there was any evil intent. He probably carries the thing for protection."

"That's generous of you to be so quick to defend him, but that's not with whom I'm angry. It's Wilkins, that incompetent fool of a private investigator I hired to find out everything there is to know about this man. How could the imbecile overlook gun ownership? Guns are registered, and whether those records are public, for the money I paid, I should have been informed."

Monica saw that he was pale. The thought of the gun in the house, so close, available for use by his would-be killer, had clearly shaken him.

"The gun isn't necessarily registered," Monica pointed out. "There are countless illegal handguns in this country. I don't know how your investigator would find out about it without seeing it for himself if it's not registered."

Mason acknowledged the possibility with a hand gesture and took a deep breath to settle down.

Monica studied him for a moment. "So, does he shoot you with it today?"

Mason ran his hands through his hair. "No, thank God, but this is unnerving to say the least."

"What will you do?"

"I don't know." He paced the room nervously. "It's in his dresser?"

"Yes, it's behind the top, left-hand drawer."

"And you say it's loaded? How can you be sure?"

"I didn't say yet, but I would have told you that I held it in my own two hands. Trust me, it's loaded. There's a bullet in every chamber."

"Yes," Mason said, remembering now.

"Will you confront him with it?"

Mason stopped and stood still. "No. Don't say a word to him. I don't want him to know that we know about it. At least our knowledge gives us an edge. I want him out of the house and away from the gun right away. You take him out somewhere."

"Where would we go?"

"Take him to breakfast, then to the zoo or a football game, anywhere. Just be gone for the day."

"What about his review?"

"Damn. You're right. I can't afford to miss one day's opportunity to research this. Wake him and switch him over to review immediately. Make sure you set the recorders as I showed you, then take him away when he's finished."

"How will I know whether he takes the gun or not?"

"It doesn't matter. As long as he's gone from the house he can't shoot me. Take the pager. Get to a phone and call in every hour on the hour. I want to know where he is at all times."

"When should we come back?"

"I'll page you. I'm going to call the investigator and find out what I can about Fontana's gun ownership. We might learn something about the man's character from that. Then I need more time to decide what to do about the gun."

"What do you want me to tell him?"

"Tell him I've had another fatal vision, involving him of course. Make something up. I don't care what. Just don't mention guns. I don't want him jittery about it. Having a gun here scares the bloody hell out of me, but for some of these characters a gun is a security blanket. The last thing I want is to chase him away now that I've started the research. Besides, if he's a gun-type and we remove this gun, he might simply get another. I would rather know where to go to preempt the pistol if I foresee trouble with it than to have to run from something coming at me from God-knows-where."

They stood silently for a minute, thinking of other issues to resolve before acting.

"The quiet here today will give me a chance to thoroughly review his recordings from last night too. Go now. Wait for my page."

Monica had hoped to stop the playful interaction with Paul, mainly through avoidance rather than confrontation. That wasn't going to work today. She wondered how she'd keep the hot-blooded man at bay when alone with him for so long.

Chapter 8

Paul was happy to leave the house with Monica. Brooks gave him the creeps with his wild eyes, hokey fantasies and science lectures. And virtually anything was better than daytime television.

After waking him, Monica assisted in his hour-long non-REM review. He found the melodious hums and vibrations relaxing, but when he saw nothing and felt no different afterward, he was again comforted and confident that the notion of dreaming the future was as silly as when he'd first heard it.

Monica explained that she was to escort him from home until further notice because of another of Mason's ominous visions.

Whatever.

With his job at the dealership behind him, Paul was game for anything. Being paid to waste time was a good thing. He hoped Brooks didn't wake up or succumb to the men in the white suits too quickly.

Their first stop was a small cafe downtown for eggs and coffee. The conversation was light and easy. Paul made an effort to be gentlemanly. He felt bad about his earlier behavior with Monica, flirting with a married woman. Not good. He'd tried to kiss her only hours after meeting her. What was he thinking? Good way to get yourself killed, Fontana.

Remember your own rules to live by: let the customer fill the silence, don't bluff with a pair of deuces, drink no cheap Scotch, and never mess with another man's woman.

After some debate on what to do, he agreed to a shopping trip to a mall across town, but only if he drove the car. Once behind the wheel, though, he drove in the opposite direction of the mall, refusing to answer Monica's protests even after pulling into the parking lot at his apartment building. Her worried look made him smile. The teasing ended when he got out, tossed her the keys, and opened the garage door to his Corvette.

"Let's drive a real car," he said.

The day was sunny and warmer than average for November. Paul removed the "T-tops" from the car and they drove the long way across town to the mall with the cool air whipping their hair in the warm autumn sun.

As a well-dressed bachelor, Paul didn't despise clothes shopping as other men often do. He was knowledgeable about both men's and women's fashions, and he enjoyed impressing Monica with his taste and expertise. She nagged him on his free spending, though, and when she suggested that she buy him some outfits, they argued for an hour, walking half the mall from shop to shop. She won the dispute in the end by explaining that she was spending Mason's money and that it should be considered living expenses for the research program.

Spending Mason's money was just fine.

They enjoyed lunch at an Italian restaurant in the mall, where they managed to find topics they could discuss for an hour without quibbling. After lunch they visited several jewelry stores, where they discovered a common interest. Paul found himself enjoying their time together, just hanging with a woman, not chasing, none of the stresses or phoniness of dating, simply being himself.

Unless he was misreading her, Monica, too, was loose and having a good time.

As agreed, she called in and spoke with Mason every hour. The calls Paul overheard were brief and cryptic. Repeatedly, Mason asked that they stay away from home until later.

"What did I kill him with this time," Paul asked Monica after one call, "slow poison?"

In a mid-afternoon call to Mason, when the fun day was beginning to drag on, Paul heard Monica claim that she was nearly out of gas in the car, as if that would prompt Mason to allow them home sooner. Why had Monica failed to tell Mason she and Paul had stopped at his apartment and were now driving the Corvette? Why should it matter?

Somehow he suspected it might.

Later in the afternoon, with clouds and colder weather moving east and the sun dropping in the west, Paul recommended they switch back to Monica's hardtop car parked at the apartment. They rode the thirty-five-mile distance in silence. Monica sat with her head back, eyes closed, and hair blowing about.

Paul used the opportunity to closely study her face with several dangerously long, eyes-off-the-road looks.

Beauty. There should be a better word.

The trouble started when they arrived at the apartment building. Paul pulled into the garage and started walking across the lot toward the apartments. Monica had turned toward her car and now stopped.

"Come on in," he said.

"No." She had that worried look again.

"What do you mean, 'no.' Does Mason want us back yet?"

"No, not yet."

"Well, where else are we going to go? My legs are killing me and my fish need to eat. Let me at least drop off these shopping bags."

Paul could see warning signs flashing in Monica's eyes. Her legs were rooted, but he persisted. "Look at your watch. You'll need to call Mason in a few minutes. May as well do it from here." Without waiting for an answer, he turned toward the building.

She shrugged and followed him.

Inside the door to his apartment, Paul sank the ten-foot shot

into the planter with his keys and kicked off his shoes, pointing
for Monica to do the same. He hauled the bags into the bedroom
and yelled out for her to make herself comfortable.

When he returned to the living room to feed the fish, Monica
was at the phone in the kitchen, calling Mason. She spoke almost
immediately after dialing the number; Mason must have
answered the phone on the first ring.

"You seem anxious," she said into the phone.

Paul wished he could hear Mason's side of the conversation.

"This is becoming a bore," Monica continued. "When can we
come home?"

More silence. Monica's forehead was slowly scrunching as she
listened.

"Seven o'clock?" she said. "Why so late?"

Mason had a lot to say this time. Monica shook her head.

Her next statement completely surprised Paul.

"We're still at the mall," she said, "and my feet are killing me."

He'd suspected that her comment to Mason earlier about gas in
the car was a lie, but this was clearly untrue.

As Mason did more talking, she twice held the phone out at
arm's length and stared at it in disbelief. Then she suddenly hung
up on him, banging the receiver hard.

When she turned around it was obvious she hadn't known that
Paul was standing in the living room feeding his fish. Her face
flushed with anger and embarrassment.

Paul dropped another pinch of food into the tank and watched
the bettas stab at it, their bodies darting and bobbing, propelled
by colorful, flowing fins.

"Why did you lie to your husband?"

"I didn't lie to him," she said, turning away.

"Come now. If you lie to me, too, I'll think you lie all the time.
You don't lie all the time, do you?"

He could feel her watching him now as he leaned down, tapping the aquarium glass and studying the fish. His attention was
fixed squarely on her, though his eyes didn't show it. You're an

arrogant bastard, Fontana, he thought, smiling at the fish.

"I don't know why I did it, really," she said, filling the silence. "I suppose I thought he would think it odd that we're here together. He has enough on his mind already."

"So you lied for his own good."

"Stop it."

"He sent you off with me for the day. What does he expect?"

"He doesn't expect us to rush over to your apartment together and..."

"And what?"

"Quit playing games with me. Mason gets jealous just like any man."

"Jealous? What's he got to be jealous about?"

"He sees the way you look at me."

"Did he tell you that?" He moved slowly past her now into the kitchen and mixed two drinks for them as she stood leaning against the counter, coiling and uncoiling the phone cord.

"No. Yes. What difference does it make? Men stare at me all the time. Of course he notices these things."

"But you think you've got to protect him from this?"

"Stop with the psychiatry."

"He's a big boy. Why not let him deal with his phobias on his own, that is, unless..." Let it go, Fontana.

He pressed a drink into her hand and she took it, barely aware she was doing so. "Unless what?"

He tried to hold himself back, but couldn't. The answer squirted out. "I just thought for a minute that maybe you were trying to steer him away from knowing about something that you secretly wanted to happen."

"You pompous pig." Her jaw stayed open.

Paul held up his hand in a peace gesture and walked into the living room, speaking over his shoulder. "Not that I'd blame you, of course."

"You conceited fool," she said, following him.

"So you deny it?"

"Of course I do," she said.

He sat on the sofa in the same spot he'd been in when she first visited his apartment. She quickly sat near him, but stayed sitting near the edge, half turned toward him to talk directly at him.

"I'm not suggesting that you're necessarily attracted to me," Paul said. "I think from the circumstances it could as easily be a negative reaction to the way your husband treats you. I'm simply here as a matter of coincidence, or convenience, trapped in the right place at the wrong time, or vice-versa. Either way, I'm sure to end up a victim."

Monica took a large gulp of her drink and shook her head. "I don't believe this."

"Tell me that your husband treats you the way you deserve. Go ahead."

Monica opened her mouth as if to do just that, but after a pause, only shook her head slowly.

"My point exactly," Paul said, touching her upper arm with the back of his hand as if they were buddies talking at the bar. "See, this old guy treats you like a thing. You don't have to be around you two for an hour to figure that out. Anyone can see it. And he talks to you badly. You didn't hang up on him here a minute ago because he was telling you how much he loves you, right?"

Monica's silence answered for her.

"There it is. See, this guy isn't treating you right. He's watching over you, always telling you what to do, and this jealousy thing, that's crazy. Wanting you? Hell yes! Who wouldn't? But owning you? You're a beautiful wildflower. Nobody owns a wildflower."

Monica turned away and started to cry.

"Oh boy. I didn't mean to make you cry." He set down his drink and took her hand. Playing your cute game, he thought, and now look what you've done.

She downed the last of her drink and set her glass down too. She wiped her eyes with her free hand, still allowing Paul to hold her other.

"Oh," she sighed, trying to compose herself, "You just don't know."

"We've got time. Why don't you tell me about it?"

"I've kept secrets for so long," she said. "I'm ashamed of what my marriage has become." She raised her hands and made the "quotes" sign with her fingers when she said the word marriage. Paul didn't follow that. "What do you mean, 'marriage?'"

"It's all related to Mason's research," she rambled on, teary eyed, "and that's secret too. I have no support network, living in a new city, away from my family, our age difference, it's too much. And with the research, we never do any socializing. I have no close friends anymore, no one to talk to. I don't know why I should keep it all bottled up any longer."

Paul saw that he'd guessed correctly about there being something wrong between Mason and Monica, but it was still a complete mystery.

"He's so cruel," she said, sobbing openly now.

"Mason?" What had Paul started here?

"How could someone do that to a person? He used me."

"How?"

"He tricked me. I'm nothing but the product of an experiment. He used his ability to brainwash me into believing I loved him. Who wouldn't? I mean, the guy could see the future. He always knew what was going to happen. He was always right. He knew how I felt and what I'd say before I even did. I was naive, sure, but how could anyone have seen this coming? How many people can do this? None. He flattered me and swarmed over me, lavishing me with gifts and affection. I thought he was God! What a fool I was."

Paul handed her a tissue. "You can't blame yourself."

"I thought we were in love. It's been a slow process, but as I learned more about these dreams of his, I realized what he'd really done. He never loved me. He lusted after me, coveted me, yes, but not love. I'm nothing but a plaything to him, a possession. He saw something he wanted and he stalked me as surely as a rapist stalks coeds from a campus bush. I feel so disgusted. I've been sleeping with a rapist for over a year. Now that he's worried he'll lose me, it's not jealousy he's feeling; he's protecting his assets."

Paul put a comforting arm around her and pulled her to his chest. "That's pretty low all right."

"I hate him."

"So you believe these dreams of the future are real?"

"Paul, it takes a while for it to sink in, but there's no question about it. He made an incredible discovery. He really is a brilliant man, but he chose to use his research as a prop to falsely impress me."

"Like falsies on the brain."

She laughed and wiped her tears again.

He took her chin in his hand and turned her toward him. Looking down into her eyes he asked, "Why don't you divorce him?"

"Haven't you heard a word I've said?" she asked.

That hurt. He thought he was doing unbelievably well as a listener up to this point. He shrugged a 'huh?'

"You dummy," she said. "We're not married. I'm Monica Westfield, not Brooks."

Paul couldn't speak for a moment. He'd felt this way once before: the time he filled a jack-high straight flush in a five-card draw poker game—all natural. It was a good feeling.

Not married. That explained it. Nothing had seemed to fit between those two, and never would. He'd been right all along. He could stop feeling guilty for his earlier behavior, and now there would be no holding back.

But just like what followed the initial rush of seeing the flush, he felt a letdown. The flush came in a game of quarter-bet-limit among friends; the reward was minuscule for all that beauty. Now, realizing that Monica was legally unattached, he faced the fact that she still lived with another man and had yet to show real interest in Paul.

"What will you do now?" he asked.

She thought for a long time.

What was there for her to do but leave him? Paul thought. How could Mason's needs possibly matter to her any longer? Then he recalled the favorite saying of a fellow salesperson at the dealership, a belief shared when discussing politics, that America was failing because at vote time "principle trips over practicality."

Perhaps it wasn't Mason's needs she had to consider. She did have a lot at stake. And was he any different? If principle ruled his actions, he'd have left the Brooks home and the whole goofy arrangement long ago.

Ah, but the money.

She closed her eyes and answered. "I have no idea what to do."

The last thing Paul could remember himself thinking before the hormones took over was that maybe he could help her decide. Then suddenly he was leaning in toward her again, and his lips were on hers. She stiffened on reflex and positioned her arms on his biceps to push him away, but she hesitated. Her lips and body remained tensed and prepared to reject him, but a moment passed. She didn't do it. His lips worked at hers. They were warm. They were soft. She smelled like a woman should smell. Still she was stiff in his arms, as if her hesitation didn't count and she could still repel him without injury to her reputation, but slowly her grip released and she began to wither. His practiced lips separated hers and their tongues met in a warm and romantic dance.

An energy began a slow burn in him, starting high and moving down his spine like fire on a wick. Then it flashed and exploded into his torso and limbs. She had him aflame like never before. The sofa and the apartment and then the world disappeared, and Paul was alone with Monica.

Chapter 9

When Mason finished his review the next morning, his stomach boiled and his pulse raced. This was not going to be a good day. The worst of it was, though he knew what was coming, he didn't know how to respond.

First things first, he thought. He called the investigator. The first dream he'd had was about the conversation they were to have later that morning. Now knowing what much of the conversation was about, he couldn't wait to hear the rest. Roger Wilkins answered his phone to a verbal barrage from Mason.

"Why the hell didn't you tell me last night?"

"Tell you what?" The investigator had just risen from bed and had no idea that Mason could now know what he wouldn't be told until later in the day.

"They went to his apartment, didn't they?"

"So she told you?"

"Absolutely not. She lied to me."

"How did you find out then?"

"I have Caller I.D." He hadn't really checked the unit for last night's call, but knew it was there now, only using it as an excuse for his knowledge. "Why didn't you tell me last night?"

The private eye paused. "Mister Brooks, why don't you come down and meet me at my office?"

"To hell with that. Answer me. I hired you to follow Monica and that gigolo. They were driving around in that sex-machine car of his and end up spending hours together at his apartment when she says they're at some shopping mall. And you don't tell me about it until the next day? First you botch the matter of the handgun, now this."

"Mister Brooks, I explained that I thoroughly checked for any record of weapons ownership on Mister Fontana, though you didn't instruct me to, and there is none. I can't know about an unregistered gun unless I see it myself, and I didn't. As for your wife, understand that eighty percent of my business involves trailing spouses suspected of infidelity. I've learned over the years not to be an accomplice to murder. With all due respect, because I'm sure this doesn't apply to you, I have a strict policy against any disclosure that might jeopardize life. Which means I don't tell some jealous guy his wife's on the way home after just sleeping with some stranger. That tends to promote domestic violence, if you know what I mean. In your case, I didn't actually witness adulterous behavior, but since I knew she'd told you they were shopping, I knew she was lying, and when an attractive young wife lies from the apartment of an equally attractive young man, my experience is that it's not to hide the fact that she's there to view his baseball card collection. We're talking hanky-panky here. I intended to call you down and tell you about it later this morning."

"Yes, I know all that. What else did you find out?"

Wilkins read from his notes about what he saw the evening before as he followed Monica and Paul. There was nothing else of significance.

Mason's first reaction was to tell Wilkins to immediately begin twenty-four-hour surveillance of Monica, but changed his mind. He paused and considered asking more about the legalities of unregistered handguns. Instead, he thanked him tersely and relieved him of further duty before hanging up the phone.

Mason leaned back in his chair and rocked gently. Must calm down, must control the temper, must think. What should he say to Monica or Paul? Should he say anything at all? Whatever action he takes, it must not jeopardize the research of Paul's dreams. He took a deep breath and the temper seemed to cool, yet his thoughts were those of an angry man pushed to the limit.

A theory had formed in Mason's head over several months, just a concept, a side-effect of his research as unbelievable as the notion of dreaming the future, and with potential for danger to society greater than drug abuse, war, disease, and famine together.

Nearly a hundred years earlier, the now-famous Viennese physician, Doctor Sigmund Freud, developed the basic tenets of psychology and psychoanalysis. One tenet states that the human mind consists of three fundamental parts: the ego, the superego, and the id. The ego is the conscious mind, directing ordinary thoughts and behavior, functional and executive in nature. The superego is more legislative and judicial, establishing the values, ideals, and prohibitions that stand as guidelines for the ego, punishing with guilt and rewarding with pride and self-esteem as appropriate. The id is the unconscious mind, harboring all instincts and all thoughts and emotions a person represses.

In the id reside powerful and potentially dangerous forces: fear, love, sexual drive, the will to survive—and the 'fight or flight' mechanism, the action-oriented response to fear and threats to love or survival. Psychosis can be the result of a breakdown in the strong barrier among the id and ego and superego. Criminal behavior, sexual deviance, and violence are thought to be linked to an overstimulated id early in childhood, or a weakened id boundary of some other cause. Such intrapsychic conflicts may cause behavior as harmless as a slip of the tongue, the 'Freudian slip,' or as deadly as homicide.

Mason knew that the sleep state is thought to temporarily weaken the intrapsychic boundaries, allowing disturbing wishes and powerful urges to slip from the id into the ego, prompting warnings to flow from the superego. This intrapsychic soup manifests itself in dreams, and when the id launches a full-scale invasion, nightmares.

Mason's theory held that his study of non-REM sleep, a breach of the subconscious mind and a portal into the future, may inadvertently open a window to the id itself. The benefits to humankind if that were true were immeasurable. Doctors could delve into the subconscious of the sick and criminally insane and eventually tinker with their deviant tendencies, possibly ending crime and mental illness forever. However, if the wall was porous and the id, through repeated crossings, learned to scale the wall with little stimulation—as happens with non-REM dreams—the result would be a world filled with psychotics, millions of egos overrun by an army of unleashed super-id's. Mason first speculated on this after being surprised by the graphic sex and violence experienced in his non-REM and, later, his REM dreams. Recently he had experienced what he thought to be an increase of potent emotions and urges in his conscious state. His reaction to situations that angered him seemed to generate feelings and ideas that were not normally part of his response repertoire.

The anger flare he felt now and the ideas floating in his head brought this theory to mind. It could be, too, that his temper was simply the result of his high stress level, with his life in danger and ongoing marital problems. It would be an exciting subject for further study, but not until after he had solved the mystery of his bond with Paul Fontana.

In a masochistic way he was proud of his cleverness for having acted upon his suspicion of Paul and Monica. After all, there hadn't been much to go on. Paul's desires were clear, but would he act on them? Monica had done only two things to make him question her faithfulness. She was quick to defend Paul on the question of the gun, and the fact that she searched his room and found the gun began to eat at Mason. What motivated her to do that? The idea to purposely delay their return home the night before and have the private eye tail them was spontaneous and just short of genius. He laid the trap, and they failed the test.

He reached in a desk drawer and pulled out the notarized original of his last will and testament. The straightforward, simple will he constructed at home with the aid of a personal-computer-based software program granted his entire estate to his beloved Monica. With a wry smile he scrolled the word 'VOID' in large block letters across all pages and initialed and dated each. He wrote a small note to himself on a post-it to have his attorney discard the only other copy kept on file, and a reminder to create a new one when he found time in the weeks ahead. He returned the now-voided will to the drawer where Monica was instructed to look upon his death. I won't even tell her, he thought. That'll surprise the little gold-digger when I pass on.

Short of that, he could think of nothing constructive to do about the situation with Paul and Monica, choosing to do nothing but bide his time, silent with the knowledge of their intimate secret, silent with his pain and anger.

He rose and headed downstairs, wondering what face to wear, and driven by the curiosity of what faces the guilty parties themselves would choose to wear.

Chapter 10

Paul woke with a smile. The previous evening's sexual encounter with Monica had continued throughout the night in his dreams. Their vivid realism was pleasantly surprising. The future, too, looked especially rosy this day. He did more than 'get lucky' the night before; he was intimate with a very special someone, and the prospects for more of the same were high. He felt something for her unlike anything he felt for a woman before. The thought of falling in love made him smile. He was too much the bachelor to get snared so quickly. She's still involved, he reminded himself. He kept smiling anyway.

Controlling a situation beyond control held a big thrill for Paul, like the thrill of blackjack or rolling the dice or letting it all ride on red at roulette and not being able to lose. Like the rare days at the dealership when he felt invincible, as if some otherworldly power had descended upon him and made him king for the day. He could sell more cars on such a day than he could in a normal week. That's how he felt today. It was the gambler's high, and he planned to run a gambit later that he couldn't lose.

First, though, there were questions he had for Monica, and more than questions if she were in the mood. He glanced at the clock on the wall. She was a few minutes late to set him up for review.

He brushed his teeth and had just returned to bed to wait her out under the covers, mostly naked, when she knocked softly on his door and slowly opened it, poking her head in.

"Are you up?" she asked quietly.

"You're way late. That's unlike you." He watched her enter the room and close the door as if she wanted her presence kept secret.

"How would you know that about me?" She moved directly to the table full of equipment and methodically began setting up the non-REM review process without looking Paul in the eye.

"I know all about you. You've been on time your whole life, haven't you?"

She shrugged, obviously distracted.

Paul was crestfallen. She was avoiding him. He felt panicky. Just when he thought everything was going his way, something was wrong. "You feel guilty about last night." He said it as it occurred to him.

After a dreadful pause she turned and faced him. "I don't know what to feel."

"Well, come here. I'll show you what to feel." He started to lower the blanket, but stopped when he saw she really wasn't in the mood. He wouldn't be able to schmooze his way with her now. Communicate with her, he thought. Tell her how you feel. She's confused about all this, and deservedly so. God, please don't let this one get away.

He said nothing for a minute and watched her fumble with the equipment. Her hands were shaking.

"About last night," he said.

"Please don't."

"I have to. I have to tell you how I feel. I can see you're having second thoughts. You feel guilty about what happened. Don't worry about what others think. They don't know your situation. Your happiness should be your concern. Something happened last night. Hell, it happened the moment I saw you. I'm afraid to even say what I think it might be, but I damn well know it isn't dirty or wrong or something that lasts only a few hours. I've never felt this way."

Monica started to cry softly. Paul sat up and took her hand.

"Tell me there wasn't something there for you last night too. Tell me you're not attracted to me and that wasn't the best love-making you've had, maybe forever. Tell me that Mason isn't so bad and that you really should stay with him and make a go of it for appearance's sake. Tell me it can't happen again and I'll quietly pack my things and I'll be out of here in five minutes. I'll never bother you again."

As Paul spoke, he slowly tugged on her arm, trying to draw her near. At first she resisted. He said his piece and then waited. For two minutes she stood silently, weakly countering the force of his pull. Paul stared hard into her teary, confused eyes. Then she caved in.

She fell into him. They embraced and their lips met in a warm and sensual kiss. Her hands explored his backside. "Yes, I felt it too," she said. They kissed long and hard. "And Mason is a scoundrel." Then she pulled away and stood with her back turned. "But you don't understand."

"Understand what?"

"I can't do this to him."

"What do you owe him after what he's done to you?"

"I can't abandon him now, not like this, not with his research so close, not with his life in the balance." Her eyes darted about the room, landing everywhere but on Paul.

There was something about women that Paul could never understand. They were so unpredictable. Just when a situation seemed so logical and clear, a woman had another way of looking at it. In past relationships he lost his patience and said and did things at times like these that he later regretted. Stay with her on this, he thought. Don't lose her.

"What is it, Monica?" he asked softly. "There's something else here. It doesn't make sense for you to stay with him and help with this little science project of his, the one that he used on you. It's okay to leave him, you know; this is the twentieth century. Or is it me?"

Monica turned and held his face in her hand. "That's right, it's you. We have to stay and follow through on the research because if Mason's life is in danger, yours may be too. He needs my assistance. There isn't time to train someone else. He hasn't even written any of this down. Whatever he's done to me is a small matter compared to the threat to your life. I can settle with him later. Mason mustn't know about us. You can't expect him to act rationally if he were to find out. What man could? He may throw you out, and then where would we be on the research? Don't you see?"

"Not at all. The guy sees the future. How's he not going to know? I assumed he already knows, that he's been sitting down the hall on his bed, pouting about losing his squeeze toy."

"No, you don't understand. He doesn't see the whole future. He only knows or sometimes has an inkling about things that will happen to him that day. If he isn't going to see it, feel it, or hear it sometime during the day, he can't foresee it by reviewing his non-REM dreams. He can only guess what goes on in other people's lives, or in their minds. Unless, of course, you tell him."

"I'd like to."

"I wouldn't. You stand to lose quite a bit if you do. If he evicts you and stops studying your dreams, your two thousand per week ends and your life could be in danger. You still have an apartment and a nice car, but no job to support them."

"And I'd lose you too?"

"I'm afraid so."

"I can play it any way you want, but I'd like to know that if I stay and keep my mouth shut and be a good boy, that you and I can still...you know...be together whenever possible, keeping an eye on something in the future."

"We've only known each other a few days."

"I just want to know there are possibilities that we're working toward."

"I don't know what the future holds for us. If you want to hold out hope, that's up to you. Mind you, though, don't you slip up and give away what's happened."

"The thought of you living with him drives me nuts."

"He's my..."

The sentence hung, unfinished. She was going to say "husband," he was sure, but realized midstream it was no longer a valid defense.

"He's a lecher." He finished for her.

Monica wagged a finger at him and completed the review setup.

"How far into the day can he see?" Paul asked, confused by the limitations of Mason's super powers.

"What do you mean?"

"You say he only dreams what will happen the next day. What time of the next day or night does that end? Does he see everything that happens each day no matter how late he stays up, or is there a set time that the crystal ball shuts down each night?"

"I see what you mean. Yes, he's seen a pattern. That's a perceptive question, Paul."

"I'm more than just hair and charm."

That earned a smile. Monica completed the equipment setup and stood over Paul, ready to attach headphones and the muscle-stimulating devices that helped elicit dream recall. "Mason's gotten so that he religiously goes to bed at nine o'clock sharp. His ESP ability apparently wears off shortly after that time. It seems based on a fixed number of hours of foresight, since he's always risen each morning at the same time. If he stays up later, the ESP fades quickly. With his life in danger, he never stays up past that point anymore."

This fascinated Paul. "So, after nine p.m. it's like a gray area where the present starts blending into the future. If he doesn't get into non-REM, the future is a surprise."

"Interesting, isn't it?"

"I'll say. He has a weakness, an Achilles' heel."

Monica was about to set the headphones over his ears, but held up and looked at Paul, puzzled.

"All you have to do," he explained, "is catch him after nine and he has no idea what you'll say or do. He's mortal just like you or me then."

Monica looked thoughtful as she finally lowered the headphones over his ears and pressed a few switches to begin the replay/review process. Before leaving the room she leaned over Paul and spoke into his covered ear. "Remember, be a good boy, or else."

After she left, Paul lay in bed thinking about their conversation. Monica was right about jealous men being unpredictable. He would have to be discreet to continue collecting the big money. A man like Mason, though, wouldn't rashly risk his life over a matter of money alone, or so Paul intended to gamble. For now, Paul relaxed and allowed the vibratory sensations and faint humming sounds of the review to take him to a far off place.

Chapter 11

Monica stood in the hall outside Paul's room, not knowing where to go. A familiar demon was crawling up her backside: desperation. With dizzying speed her life was crumbling, an existence with a plan and structure as tenuous as a hastily-crafted sand castle, now suddenly washed away by a force beyond her control.

This was her greatest fear come true. All her life she had run from the truth—the great proclamation by her father that she could do no right. Try as she might through the years to prove she could make decisions and direct her life, his warnings now loomed prophetic. It seemed like she had never received positive words from him on anything she did as a child, and his attacks negated any praise and encouragement offered by her mother. As a result, she really never knew whether she was on the right track with anything. Her leaving home, college years, relationship with Mason—everything—had been a series of panic-driven dart-throws. There was no plan, not even a goal other than creature comfort. The darts appeared to have landed well, earlier. Indeed, there was happiness and wealth, but now it was all falling apart.

She couldn't return to her family in Buffalo. She didn't work, and had no training or skill. She had dropped out of college at Mason's urging. Her "marriage" was failing. Now she was falling for an underemployed and oversexed car salesman. Constantly the bizarre and frightening threat posed by the research was on her mind. The two closest people in her life were marked for death by some unknown power.

If this fell apart, where would she go? What would she do? How would she live?

She paced the long Oriental rug that ran the full length of the hallway's hardwood floor, passing between a pair of matching oak pedestals that supported antique vases. Mason was likely in the kitchen now, preparing his daily cappuccino, between completing his review and starting Paul's. She wasn't yet ready to face him. Her room a few doors down the hall offered temporary refuge, a place she could hide and consider her next steps.

She lay back on her bed and stared unseeing at the intricate lace canopy overhead. The role as 'wife' of Mason Brooks was so easy when all decisions were black and white. Do you want an exciting career and riches? Say yes. Do you want eternal love and happiness? Say yes. Do you want to be cared for by one of the world's most brilliant and capable men? Say yes.

Want for nothing ever again.

It was easy to forget that her status was a charade, that she had achieved nothing on her own merit. Father said she would have to cash in on her good looks to get anywhere in this world. Admitting he was right hurt more than her disintegrating life.

Think. What are the options here? Leaving was out of the question. There was nowhere to go, and once there, nothing to spend.

She was forced to face the issue she'd been dodging: what were her motives here? Truthfully, from the start, Mason's wealth made choosing him easier, but that wasn't at the heart of it. She fought hard to disprove her father's contention that it would, in the end, be a "sugar daddy" who saved her. No, she truly and naively moved in with Mason under more idealistic motives. Now, though, with the end of the ride in sight, the thought of financial insecurity and a future without prospects daunted her. Even so, she knew she had the fortitude to face it if need be. But why should it be so?

After what Mason had done to her, she deserved a share of his wealth, and he deserved to part with it. Greed didn't enter into it; need and retribution did.

Unfortunately, she couldn't trust Mason to share if they were estranged. If married, divorce offered a chance at a good portion of his money, but that would take time and she couldn't win if he decided not to play fair with the finances. One way or another he would use his powers to short her in the proceedings. The wealth, too, wasn't so much an enormous number of millions as it was the bottomless potential offered by Mason's ability. It declined over recent months as they binge-spent and the bond distracted Mason from replenishing it. Also, the half or less she could have expected in divorce would be dangerously thin as sole support for a lifetime.

It was easy to acclimate oneself to this lifestyle, and hard to give it up. With no foreseeable means of self-support in future years, she would have to come away with big money in any split with Mason. She had no confidence that could be done now.

Paul Fontana was attractive and exciting, but that paid no bills. She'd held off the horny hordes for years and could do so longer if need be. The priority was a financial foundation, a portfolio in her name, enough money to allow her to forget her own short-comings.

There were only two ways to get that kind of money. One she had control over and was the logical course of action: tough it out with Mason for more months and influence him to increase their wealth to safer levels while tactfully promoting the idea of shar-ing his wealth when they split—a quasi-post-nuptial agreement.

The other was Mason's death, an event beyond her control, but one that would leave his entire estate willed to her. Fate was flex-ing its muscles, wasn't it? She couldn't keep from her mind the thought that this seemingly imminent event now represented opportunity rather than tragedy. Her wait may not be long.

Mason was unaware of her affair with Paul, and would stay that way as long as Paul kept his mouth shut. Mason obviously felt the strain in their relationship, but his aim was to continue it.

Monica was providing the pull-apart as Mason's actions sickened her more and more. That was something she could shelve temporarily.

She pulled a pillow over her face and sighed into it, committing herself to the awkward task of playacting the happy and supportive wife for untold weeks to come. Somehow she must convince Mason to find the time to win more money in the market or at the track.

Paul Fontana must be held in check. Having had a taste, he would be rabid with lust, and would spoil her only chance at security if his loose tongue caused Mason to expel them both in a rage. It was hard not to believe the threat to Mason's life was real, but difficult to imagine him solving the mystery and deflecting his doom; he had no idea what he was looking for. The notion occurred more than once to Monica that his having invited an armed Paul Fontana into his home could be the action that ultimately sealed his fate. She tried to avoid consciously thinking that Paul should stay in the home for that reason.

She threw the pillow aside and checked the clock on the nightstand. Mason was probably still downstairs, waiting for Paul to finish his review and wondering where she was. She couldn't bring herself to go down alone. A key element of success over the weeks to come would be strategic avoidance. She'd wait to go downstairs until Paul concluded his review and she prepared it for Mason. Maybe if Paul was present, she could avoid Mason's eyes.

It occurred to her, too, that avoiding Mason was going to be easier than avoiding Paul. She would be chaperoning a wolf for hours daily, one she had encouraged and also felt a strong attraction to. This was going to be messy, but there was no other choice.

Chapter 12

Mason descended the stairs deep in thought, with one hand rubbing the banister and the other in his pants pocket. Today's forecast was another bad one, and events were confirming it early. No matter what might come later, it would surely be over-shadowed by the revelations acquired from the investigator. His review of Paul's non-REM recording had proved fruitless. Now he had to face the two conspirators and get through the day as if nothing had happened. When was something going to go right?

The intriguing question of whether he might someday foresee his review of Paul's review with his own review—thereby saving the hour it took to do it for real—was on his mind as he entered the kitchen and dining area. That led to other unanswerable questions on the makeup of the universe and time and space and the interrelationships of all people and things.

He shook his head and sighed. Focus, and forget the rest. Focus on the bond. One good thing there, surprisingly, was that in the three days Paul Fontana had been in the house, gun and all, a move Mason deliberated long and hard, there had been no premonitions of death. Was there a connection?

There were so many questions.

Paul sat at the oak table, feeding on three scrambled eggs, sausage links and buttered toast. He barely looked up when Mason walked in.

Monica faced the counter, cooking Mason's breakfast. She

threw a quick glance over her shoulder at him as he entered the room. "Almost done, dear," she said cheerfully, "Have a seat. Say, how is the day looking? I've got a few things I'd like to take care of on my own. I was wondering if Paul could tend to himself today, or were there more problem dreams last night?"

Mason almost smiled with disgust. That's clever. Disguise your interest with disinterest. He was about to answer her question with a few of his own, but caught a glimpse of Paul's face out of the corner of his eye and it froze him.

When Mason didn't answer her, Monica turned to look, saw him staring at Paul, looked at Paul, and then she, too, stood gawking at the peculiar look on Paul's face.

Paul sat motionless, staring past them, trance-like, his arm suspended in midair with a skewered sausage link poised for biting off his fork. He shuddered and shook his head as if casting off a spell.

"Wow," he said, now looking startled as his eyes came back to focus. "Deja vu, man. That was incredible. I've never felt anything like that before. I mean, I've had deja vu before, but not like that. It was so real." He looked up at Monica. "I knew exactly what you were going to say. If I'd thought about it and got my mouth open sooner, I could have said it before you did."

Mason stamped his foot and pounded his fist into an open hand. He knew what this meant: success!

Monica looked from Paul to Mason and back and forth several more times, her mouth open, the spatula dripping pork grease on the linoleum. "Could it be?" she asked Mason.

"Absolutely, it could be," he said, pacing and speaking with animated arm gestures. "It must be. I know the feeling well. This is what I would have expected."

Monica pointed the spatula at Paul, who had just realized he was still holding his sausage in the air and dropped his arm to the table. "How could it have worked on him so fast?" she asked. "It took you months." There was a hint of concern in her voice, as if the unbelievable were suddenly proven possible again.

"That was because my early procedures were trial and error. I had no idea how to set up the equipment. I've learned all that over time. This is what should happen. In fact, it should happen sooner; a subject—any subject—should feel these same results after only one review. When I get this process to the optimal point, that is. Obviously, there's still tweaking to be done."

"What does this mean?" Monica asked.

"For one, it's confirmation that this non-REM phenomenon is not limited to me. There's nothing inherently unique about Mason Brooks; this happens to everyone. Second, it means the world has just experienced a paradigm shift. Life for humankind will never be the same. Ten years from now we'll have the review process refined and equipment miniaturized to the point that every home in the civilized world has a non-REM unit and billions of people spend their mornings previewing their day with a roll and a cup of coffee as nonchalantly as they now watch the morning news. We can only speculate on the changes this will mean for society—good or bad?" He shrugged.

Paul sat in stunned silence, his food getting cold.

Monica removed the skillet from the stove, shoveled the overdone eggs and sausage onto a plate, and set it aside on the counter, sure that the discussion superseded Mason's hunger. "What does this say about the relationship between Paul and your dreams?"

"Unfortunately, nothing yet. It only means he, too, can now see the future. My review of his recordings has been like lying in a vibrating bed at a cheap motel while listening to static on the radio, and about as enlightening. I suspect that my review of his data may never yield results, and that may be the nature of this. Everyone's dreams may be intelligible to them exclusively. I don't know. I'll continue, of course, but it takes so much time to do my review, then Paul's, then study and map his EEG printouts, I haven't had time to look at my own printouts. Someday I must take time to document this discovery. My review alone seems to provide me with what I need to know about the day's danger, but

I hope that overlooking my raw data doesn't come back to haunt me somehow.

"The exciting thing now is that I can interview Paul after his own reviews and he can tell me what he dreams. In that way I can see possible correlations: shared dreams or other anomalies. I can also study his electrocortigraphic readouts, and the others, and make notations as he relates his experiences each morning. I'm hopeful that an experienced technician could eventually interpret such readouts meaningfully, similar to what a seismologist, cardiologist or lie detector operator might do. That is what I've been trying to do with my own data, but that must wait now."

Monica nodded and bounced a finger off her lips pensively. Paul leaned back in his chair and locked his fingers behind his head. Sighing deeply, he appeared overwhelmed by the implications of his experience.

Mason continued. "In any event, this is progress, and that is something I have sorely missed of late." His mind was racing. Ideas of things to try and directions to take were bouncing about his cranium. He rubbed his temples. "Paul, if you consent, I'd like to prescribe a modest dosage of Nardil for you."

Paul raised an eyebrow.

"There's nothing to become alarmed about. Nardil is an innocuous antidepressant drug. It has the effect of reducing REM activity during the sleep phase—paradoxical sleep—thereby increasing non-REM activity. It has few side effects, particularly in the low dosages I'm thinking of. I've used it myself for some time now, and I find it useful in increasing dream recall and retention. We may also want to experiment with one or two psychotropic drugs that chemically alter behavioral response to see what that yields."

Paul looked to Monica, who shrugged.

"Just a wild thought," Monica said, "but what if you were to do a review of Paul's recordings while you yourself were asleep? Wouldn't that—"

"Monica," Mason interrupted, "I appreciate your willingness to contribute, but that is exceedingly silly. If you paid the least attention to your schooling and what I have attempted to teach you over the years, you would know that sleep-learning is a myth. I'm afraid that many hours have been spent in vain playing tapes or reading to sleeping college students who hoped to better their grades after a night on the town rather than a night of good old-fashioned studying."

Stung but unwilling to show it, Monica said, "I realize that, Mason, but I thought perhaps the nature of the recordings, which include the vibration and other stimuli not present in the old reading or recorded sleep-learning lessons, may in some unpredictable way influence dream response, not learning."

On second thought, the idea wasn't any more outlandish than others Mason had already experimented with. The idea might have merit, and he would probably try it at some point, but he was in no mood to concede ground to his unfaithful Monica. It might be in his best short-term interest to keep from throwing her out, but he wasn't required to play husband of the year either.

Mason waved her off rudely, and changed the subject. "In answer to your earlier question, yes, it will be fine for you to leave Paul unattended today. I've foreseen no problems there. What I will ask, though, is that while you're out you purchase the best video camera you can find, with all the accessories: tripod, AC adapter, motion-detectors, the best lens, whatever's available. And get a VCR and monitor that will allow me to do nonstop recording for up to twelve hours unattended, something like a store's security camera."

"What's that for?"

"I should have thought of it earlier, but now it's particularly relevant. I want to videotape Paul's entire night's sleep. Get the best microphone money can buy. I want to hear every word he mutters in his sleep. See if the videocams come with timers, too, so we can correlate any visual response with the other readouts. One clue I've had that non-REM sleep is more than it appears is that most sleep-walking and sleep-talking is done in non-REM stage.

This little fact has been difficult to explain for non-REM nonbelievers. If one is supposedly in a deep, non-dream state, how do you explain spontaneous walking and talking? And if, as some assert, these are responses to the recollections of a REM dream, what is one doing responding to anything in this deep-sleep, nothingness state? There's an inconsistency there. I theorize that this is a physical reaction to non-REM dreams. Sleepwalkers and talkers may be literally acting out future events. If we could see this on tape and decipher the spoken words, we'd be closer to seeing that person's future. In our case that would be extremely useful."

Paul, who had still not uttered a word since relating his deja vu episode, finally spoke. "Question. With these dreams, if you can really see the next day's...stuff, and what you don't like about it, you can change, and even the things you do like, you don't have to do because you've already done them, sort of, when do we all get to the point where we're just lying around on the couch all day, happy as could be, knowing all, and doing nothing?"

Mason smiled broadly. "Ah. I can't answer that question, but I can see, Paul, that you're beginning to appreciate my intense interest in this subject. Do you still consider me an 'old lunatic' now?"

Paul had no response.

Chapter 13

Paul checked his watch again. A few more minutes to go. The butterflies in his belly were a surprise. He passed the time sitting on the edge of his bed, spinning his bracelet around his wrist with his free hand, an age-old habit. Why was he sweating this so?

Go ahead and pretend this is no big deal, Bucko, but you know better. You're about to roll the dice like never before. Everything is riding on this one. More money than you've ever had, and the hottest woman. Maybe even your life.

There were many factors for Paul to consider in deciding on his bold plan. All of them added to the same ironic conclusion: while he stood to lose all, he had virtually nothing to lose. Financially, he risked nothing, and if Mason was right, his life was in danger either way.

He checked the watch again. Two minutes past nine p.m. Anytime now. He'd left the bedroom door ajar so he could hear into the hall. He stood and paced behind it. Sweat dripped down inside his pressed shirt. He neatly folded the cuffs back three times over his forearms and took two deep breaths.

Footsteps sounded on the staircase outside the door and his pulse jumped. Peering through the crack in the door, he saw Mason Brooks reach the top of the stairs and turn down the hall toward his bedroom and study. Paul checked the clock again to be sure. Brooks was punctual.

Let's hope Monica has her facts right.

Paul waited for Mason to reach the door at the end of the hall, then took another deep breath and went into action. Swinging open his door, he stepped into the hall and spoke forcefully.

"Mason, we need to talk."

Mason spun around and nearly stumbled, as if the bogeyman himself had jumped out of a bush and yelled 'boo.' His eyes fell immediately to his wristwatch, then back to Paul. The startled look on his face didn't improve. In the dim light of the hall, Mason Brooks suddenly looked old, vulnerable, and scared. His usual aura of superior intellect, which made Paul feel so insignificant and uncomfortable, instantly evaporated.

Paul walked directly toward him, taking bold steps. He guessed correctly what Mason's reaction would be.

Mason paled noticeably, even in the dim light. He retreated a step toward his door and held up a hand as if to repel Paul's advance. "Not now, please. Anything you have to say can wait until tomorrow."

"It can't wait."

"I'm afraid it'll have to."

Mason turned and opened his door behind him.

Undeterred, Paul followed him into the room and closed the door. They stood silently facing each other. Paul noticed Mason's hands shaking uncontrollably. He pitied Mason for this cruel mind game, but curiously Mason's fear only served to calm Paul and steel his resolve in his bold undertaking. He held his tongue a minute more, purposely dragging out the ordeal for Mason, heightening the suspense.

It gave him an opportunity to look around the room he'd not yet been inside. Mason Brooks' room was interesting. Obviously once a master bedroom, it was still decorated as such but had given way to the advancing high-tech equipment that now filled it like weeds in an untended garden. There was little planning for the organization and layout of the array, as if components were haphazardly added as money or the whim allowed. A king-size bed lay centrally, jutting on a diagonal from the far corner, surrounded by gadgets of incomprehensible purpose. Monitors hung overhead. No less than three separate keyboards lay at the foot of the bed, their spiral cords leading off in different directions into a tangled jungle of wires. Mason Brooks' 'research facility' was his bed, where he could both record and study his dream activity. If Paul's guest room looked like a well-equipped doctor's office, Mason's was an operating room or a science fiction movie set. It wasn't immediately obvious how Mason got into and out of the bed.

To his credit, Mason swallowed hard and found his voice. "I must insist, Paul, that you leave my room immediately. I follow a strict schedule as required by my research. Whatever it is you wish to discuss, I assure you, we'll set aside as much time as you require tomorrow and I'll lend you my undivided attention. Now, please." He raised his hand toward the door, an invitation for Paul to leave.

He was doing an admirable job of maintaining his dignity and holding his water, but Paul read his eyes: naked fear. Fading vision, hell. Monica had understated it. Mason had no idea what was about to happen. The fear increased Paul's chances of success, and his enjoyment too.

"This won't take long," he said, allowing a sly smile.

Mason's eyes did a once-over of Paul's body. Looking for a weapon, perhaps? With another moment of silence Mason seemed to accept the fact that Paul wasn't leaving. He planted his feet and spoke with renewed fortitude in a tone that reminded Paul of the British tradition of courage in the face of adversity, something he'd seen in old movies like The Bridge on The River Kwai.

"Well, let's have it then," Mason said matter-of-factly.

Instantly Paul developed a deep respect for the man. Probably thinking he's about to die, he stands resolute and says, "Bring it on."

Paul had a deeper respect for Mason's wealth, though. That's what we're here for, he reminded himself. Here we go.

"I've been thinking about our arrangement, and it's occurred to me that it's not quite adequate."

"Oh? How so?"

"Well, as I see it, you're a rich man whose life is in danger. Now it just so happens that I'm the only one on earth who holds the key to breaking that threat. For what at the time seemed like a generous offer of two thousand dollars per week I agreed to help with your problem. I've moved into a strange home and given up my career. I've allowed myself to be hooked to god-knows-what kinds of equipment, not having any clue about what danger that really puts me in. Now you're talking about drug experiments. I have no contract, no guarantee that the money will be paid on time, or at all. No commitment to any specific term. I could be out on my ass next week, flat broke and without a job.

"All this was a little easier to accept before this morning. Life was carefree and the money sounded better when I believed the whole thing was a big joke. I would have felt guilty for taking your money—until this morning. That's when I realized this is no game. That little episode I had this morning was...well, I think you know. It's quite a shock. It's everything you said. So now I can no longer shrug off your wild stories of death. I have to assume they're true, and as you've said, it looks sometimes as though I'm included in the plan.

"So the way I figure it, if it comes true, we're both dead and none of this matters, but if it doesn't happen, then I've played a major role in heading it off, and you get to live a long, happy and wealthy life. If that's true, then I deserve the same. You should be grateful to me to the tune of more than two thousand per week."

"To the tune of how much?"

"Twenty thousand per week, in advance. That puts you three days behind schedule on the first payment."

The look of fear in Mason's eyes changed to rage, and suddenly it was Paul's turn to question his safety. Mason was older and smaller, but the look in his eye was disconcerting nonetheless.

"You're nothing but a cheap thug," Mason said.

"Why should the amount matter to you? With your ability you can make that much every day."

"Money isn't everything, Mister Fontana. There are such things as integrity and self-respect. This was a fair deal before. You already agreed to it."

"You can't expect me to have much self-respect if I don't get the best deal I can on this. It's only natural."

"Just business, huh?"

"Why not? It looks like I'm destined for either death or riches, maybe both. I figure it's better to die rich."

Mason stared at Paul long and hard. The unpleasant feeling that Mason knew something Paul didn't was returning. For the hundredth time Paul regretted not attending college, as if then he'd know what it was that all college graduates knew that he didn't. Then maybe he could stare down the likes of Mason Brooks with confidence. For now, he faked it, his eyes staring unblinking, cold, firm. In his mind he repeated the word 'wild,' hoping the see-all Brooks would somehow read it telepathically and become fearful again.

Instead, Mason challenged, with a note of sarcasm. "And if I refuse?"

"Come on, Brooks. You have no choice. Thirty years of devoted research got you to this point. Now, not only is fame, fortune, and scientific achievement here, so is death. Money means nothing to you. Sure, maybe this pisses you off in a scumbag-black-mails-Ph.D. kind of way, but you're above all that. You've got bigger things to worry about. Part with the money."

Mason repeated the question. "If I refuse?"

"It's simple. I walk."

"What of our agreement? What about two thousand per week? What about your experience this morning? Don't you want to take it further?"

"Look, I came here with nothing and I can go away with less if that's the way you want it. It's up to you. I've got nothing to lose and you've got the world to share."

"How do you know I haven't already learned what I need to know from you?"

That caught Paul by surprise. He hesitated, then smiled. Nothing but a bluff. "We wouldn't be having this conversation if that were true. I'd have been out of here already, and we wouldn't be negotiating like we are now."

"Negotiating? That's what this is? I see, well...then I withdraw from the table for now. I no longer wish to discuss this issue further tonight. I agree to at least consider your demands and I will respond accordingly in the morning after further deliberation." He crossed his arms.

Paul was hoping on a go or no-go resolution tonight. This was unexpected. Yet, Mason left the door open for success. Paul didn't really want to leave tonight anyway. What could it hurt to stay the night and let the facts sink in to Mason? Surely he would logically conclude that capitulation was the only choice. There was no need to push the issue further tonight and possibly force a decision based on emotion, one that may go against Paul's wishes.

"I'll accept that," he said, stuffing his hands into his pockets and acting cooler than he felt.

"Excellent. I shall render my decision in the morning then."

"Fine," Paul said, not sure what Mason was up to.

"Good evening to you then." Mason again gestured toward the door.

Paul left the room more uncertain about what he'd accomplished than he hoped. He had definitely surprised Brooks, though, and that gave him an edge. Yet, Mason was damn smart. Too smart.

Chapter 14

Mason had been off to bed only fifteen minutes when Monica realized she forgot to ask him about his investigation of Paul's gun the day before. Her lack of curiosity had to seem conspicuous in its absence. Why hadn't he broached the subject? Maybe he'd been preoccupied with the day's developments and the matter slipped his mind. That would be her excuse when she asked about it tomorrow.

She considered, too, the pros and cons of broaching another subject with Mason in the morning: marriage. As distasteful as the thought of wedding Mason now seemed, the reality of how legally weak their arrangement was, sank in. Clearly Mason loved her as a possession, one he showed no interest in disposing of. But what if that changed? His love could sour if she failed to maintain the pretense of loving 'spouse,' or if he suspected her of being unfaithful. Whatever the cause, Mason could duplicate the magic he'd worked on her with other young, attractive women, and he knew it. Given enough resistance and rejection, he surely wouldn't hesitate to abandon her. She could find herself in the street in a flash. The will naming her as beneficiary could be voided with the stroke of a pen, leaving her penniless.

Marriage could protect against such a catastrophe. As she understood it, even without a will, as a spouse she stood to inherit his entire estate unless she agreed otherwise. That she would not do. She knew of cases in which jilted lovers sued for a share of net worth based on promises made, but that would be time-consuming, expensive, messy, and public, none of which appealed to her. She'd heard of court-ordered financial splits based on the concept of 'common law marriage.' Surely, though, their two-year relationship fell short of establishing a basis for that. Any notion of her garnering his prior agreement to pay her off if they split was ludicrous. He would see through her feeble attempts to achieve that. In truth, she had no protection at all. He could oust her and pay not one penny. He could also write her out of his will. With Mason dead or alive she was vulnerable. Marriage could be the ticket, though. He would be forced to share the wealth if they split, and the will would be rendered academic, as she would be named next of kin.

How would Mason receive the notion of marriage, though? Logically, all concerns about appearances in the community, university, or extended family had waned in the two years since she'd moved in with him. Most people believed they were married. They could do whatever they wanted and no one would pay the least bit of attention. A marriage could be done so privately that no one need know anyway. If she were to propose such a thing, what would her motive be? Would Mason see through it?

Monica closed the book she held open in her lap and pulled her feet up under her in the chair. She hadn't read a word in nearly an hour. The antique cherrywood clock on the mantel reminded her to prepare Paul for sleep in fifteen minutes. As the fire crackled in the stone hearth she mused at the false serenity in the quiet house. Outside, a cold wind picked up, symbolic of the turmoil flailing beneath her calm exterior.

Mason sensed the tension between them, she was sure. If he suspected her true motive behind a marriage proposal was to seek reparation, it would surely backfire. She needed to explain it in a way that seemed logical to an intelligent yet insensitive man like Mason. Something like having secretly always wanted to marry.

Then, how about: our relationship has been strained of late, but we're good together. We have too much between us to throw away. Marriage could be a way to renew our commitment to each other and take our relationship to a new level.

She could also remind him of the discord with her father. Going through life as a Westfield was no longer tolerable. She wanted to marry and assume another name and identity, something as honorable as the Brooks surname.

It sounded thin. If only she could reverse the roles and use his magic on him, give him a taste of his own medicine. Instead, that magic would work against her again. Unfortunately, Mason would wake on the day she proposed marriage knowing about it before it happened. That would afford him the chance to consider it from all angles ahead of time, eliminating the element of surprise. That time to think about it before she could press the matter in person with soft voice and warm body worried her. His analysis would be cold and calculating, and ultimately, his ability to manipulate the future could somehow prevent the proposal from ever happening if he so chose.

Paul had said something the other night, though, astutely hypothesizing that Mason had a blind spot. He could be surprised after nine p.m. Perhaps she could propose to him after he headed to the lab for his nightly ritual. If she caught him off guard without any sense of what was to come, her chances would improve. With the right performance, she could envision him falling for what he wanted their relationship to be like. That she still loved and worshiped him. Did that apply to a man who could see and change the future, though?

Monica rose to do her duty with Paul's equipment setup. Setting her book on the end table, she noticed for the first time the new book Mason had taken up that evening. She picked it up and leafed through it. It was a large coffee table book, a reference guide to handguns: a thorough rendering of available weaponry, complete with color photos, brand names, price ranges, and vital statistics. An odd selection. Whether or not he broached the subject with her, he had obviously heard something from his investigator about Paul's pistol and now had guns on the mind.

Chapter 15

Mason finished his morning non-REM review with a sick feeling. His 'gift' had become a burden. Feelings were out of control: anger, jealousy, fear, guilt. His dreams, both REM and non-REM, reflected it all. What he'd seen the night before scared him like nothing before. Yet in a way there was a sense of relief too; finally, he saw a path, a direction to follow. It was still obscure in all its finer details, but he knew they would clear up in flashes of deja vu and additional non-REM review revelations as the days progressed.

Also there was a strange sense that despite his abilities, the future was somehow chosen, locked-in, that there was no choice in how to proceed. That is, as long as logic and self-preservation were still primary motivators in his increasingly bizarre existence.

He drew a deep breath and dressed in a worn v-neck sweater he knew Monica at one time liked. In the dresser mirror he brushed his hair, carefully distributing it to minimize thin spots. Studying the lines around his eyes, he questioned whether he had the courage to follow through with his new and nebulous plan. He had to find out. The plan was logical. Like the flick of a switch, he committed himself to the attempt.

A door down the hall closed and Mason quickly leaned out of his room in time to see Monica heading down the stairs after preparing Paul's a.m. review. He called after her in as pleasant a voice as he could muster.

"Monica, darling, how long until Paul is finished?"

Monica turned and looked up the hall at him from two steps down. Even at a distance Mason saw his tone surprised her.

"In just a minute...dear."

"Will you ask him to see me in here before he goes down? I want to discuss his results first thing this morning."

She nodded, and after standing confused for a moment, retraced her steps to Paul's room.

Ten minutes later, Paul Fontana knocked on Mason's door.

"Come in, Paul."

Paul entered slowly. Without turning his head, his eyes scanned the room. "What's up?"

"I've given your proposal thought and wanted to respond first thing to try to clear this matter. I hope we can put it behind us and press on with the more important task before us."

"And?" Paul folded his arms.

"It occurs to me that you're not the type of person who is easily satisfied. What one day may seem adequate to you is the next day not enough. Witness the example before us: two thousand dollars a week was fair to you one day, later not. I have no assurance or expectation that your current demand of twenty thousand dollars per week will satisfy you for long, which leads me to the conclusion that at some point I will be unable or unwilling to afford your price. In either case, I have no desire to face this issue again. Consequently, I will no longer barter for your services on a cash-per-week basis."

"You need me, Brooks." Paul pointed a finger at him.

"As you do me, Mister Fontana, but I tire of the efforts required to convince you of that. Your small-minded money-grubbing irritates me beyond words. I want no part of it."

"We could do eighteen grand with a guarantee there'd be no more hikes."

Mason waved off the desperate negotiation. "I propose an alternative. Take it or leave it. I doubt I can make enough money to satisfy your needs, but you can. My offer is to teach you the same skills I used to acquire my wealth. It's quite simple and can be done in the next couple of days. I'm guessing your deja vu experience yesterday was enough to convince you this is truly possible. In any event, given the opportunity, I can prove it to you beyond doubt. This is not something I wanted to take time to dally with, but under the circumstances...you have me in a bit of a pickle. I want to continue our research. We've had early success, so I'm willing to postpone further research for a day or so to resolve this."

Paul rubbed the skin under his nose between thumb and forefinger. His eyebrows went together. "How exactly would it work?"

"We could start immediately, take a day of preparation and make a short trip to Atlantic City to test it. I could use more funds myself. During that trip you'll win thousands—how many is hard to say. You won't be rich, but you'll see how the process works and how in the future you can duplicate it as often as desired. I'll see that regardless of what happens to our association, you leave here with the necessary equipment to continue non-REM reviews, allowing you to capitalize as I have. This is win-win, Paul. It costs me nothing but time, and you'll have unlimited wealth."

Paul's fingers now tugged at his cheek. Mason could see the words 'unlimited wealth' rolling around in his mind. A sudden surge of deja vu confirmed his optimism. Paul liked this notion. He liked it a lot.

"That's an interesting idea," Paul said, breaking a smile. "Which casino would we visit?"

"There's a dozen. Do you have a preference?"

"Best to go to Bally's Park Place. I've spent the least time there."

"As you wish, but I need your word that after our trip we're back here and all business. You'll have the rest of your life to cash in."

"And if it doesn't work?"

"It will. If it makes you feel better, I'll agree to your twenty thousand if it doesn't."

Paul's smile now showed teeth. "Deal. When do we start?"

"After breakfast. I'll have Monica take you to the university library. Pick out every book you can find on the subject of black-jack and study it. Does blackjack suit you?"

"Yeah, fine. Any others?"

"Not now. Concentrate on one subject only, immerse yourself in it. Spend your day reading, thinking about, and if you like, playing blackjack. If we're successful, you'll have spent enough time on the game to make it the subject of both REM and non-REM dream activity tonight. If it makes it to your non-REM, we're in business, because tomorrow, after your morning review, we'll drive down to Atlantic City."

"Drive? That's four hours."

"I won't fly with you, thanks."

Paul rolled his eyes.

Mason continued. "If we're gambling in Atlantic City tomorrow afternoon, you're dreaming about it tonight in non-REM. I don't expect you to have clear foresight as you play, although you might have a few helpful deja vus. What I do expect is that if you relax and play your hunches, whether or not they appear to you as clear premonitions of card falls, you'll win an inordinate number of hands, more than the odds can explain, and enough to convince you."

"Weird."

"Quite. The big money comes later when you learn to combine the technique of lucid dreaming to optimize your possibilities."

"I don't get that part."

"On this first trip we hope to have some foreknowledge of what is already decided to happen. You capitalize on that by making conscious decisions to act, knowing what is to come."

Paul nodded.

"With lucid dreaming you become aware of the non-REM

dream as it occurs and can direct it to suit your purposes. You can't decide what to dream, but you can lead an in-progress dream in a certain direction. Since you are dreaming the future, your lucid 'changes' actually manipulate future."

"Give me an example."

"As I got better at horse betting, I not only knew which horse would win, I could affect the odds and make a horse a longshot, increasing my payout. I affected the odds by leading the non-REM dream that way with lucid dreaming."

"That's cheating," Paul said with a smile that barely fit on his face.

Mason found his crude enthusiasm humorous and laughed despite himself.

Paul scratched the top of his head. "What happens when this technology is there for everybody to use and lots of people try to manipulate the same future? Somebody's bound to lose."

"It seems there must be limits."

"Yeah. Otherwise, it's going to be tough on the casinos."

They stood in awkward silence, each pondering his own blossoming comprehension of an enigma that grew more incomprehensible with each new level of understanding.

Chapter 16

Throughout the day Paul experienced deja vu. Some episodes were faint twinges. Others, though, exceeded the breathtaking clarity of the previous morning's event. The shear number of episodes was evidence of something supernatural. The fact that the first day's breakthrough was followed by such an increase in frequency and intensity was proof to Paul that Brooks' discovery was real. Based on two days' experience, he expected each subsequent day to bestow improved extrasensory powers on him.

The profound realization that he, Paul Fontana, would shortly foresee and manipulate the future to suit his purposes pasted a persistent smile on his face. He was aglow with a sense of well being almost orgasmic in quality. For several minutes that morning he stood before the mirror, chuckling at his good fortune. It wasn't the advancement of science or the betterment of humankind at the heart of his bliss. It was money, all the money he could ever need or want. What had Brooks called it? Unlimited wealth. Yeah, maybe that's what they call it in the faculty washroom down at the university, but uptown where I live they call it something else: filthy, stinking rich.

He wanted to bathe in bills, roll in Krugerrands, pay for drinks with hundred dollar bills and leave fifty-dollar tips for cute waitresses. The nineteen eighty-four Corvette would go too, replaced by another only dreamed of: a nineteen seventy Stingray roadster with a four hundred fifty-four cubic inch 'rat' motor, four-barrel

Holly carb mounted on a high-rise manifold, high-flow air filter, electronic ignition, and a cam so hot he'd have to rev the tach to twenty-five hundred RPMs just to keep her running at stoplights. Clothes, homes, travel...the list went on.

At the top of the list of items he could soon afford was the one item money couldn't buy: Monica Westfield. He watched her from his seat in the library where he sat at a monstrous old table poring over a half-dozen books on the subject of blackjack. He was several hours into his day-long cram-session on a card game he already felt knowledgeable enough on to write his own volume. Distractions were making the going tedious.

"This is boring," he said loudly enough for Monica and others to hear. A few curious heads bobbed up.

Monica shuffled over and admonished him before returning to the shelves.

"Remember what Mason warned you about," she said. "Don't be deterred, continue to focus. After all, a day 'wasted' is a small price to pay for the reward awaiting you. As ironic as it may seem, boredom is good. It's precisely the condition to strive for when studying, since it suggests your mind is reaching saturation on the topic and is groping for other fertile matter to contemplate."

For Paul, that fertile matter was again standing twenty feet away, searching the shelves for more reading material. She had dressed down today, conservatively, casual, as if trying not to impress. She wore plain, white sneakers, worn denims, and an oversized, grey sweatshirt emblazoned with the university's name in school colors. Her black hair was drawn back into a thick, loose braid, while a judicious few strands dangled provocatively alongside her face.

Monica may have thought she was disguised as plain, but Paul considered himself a connoisseur of fine women, and on female beauty held the conviction that while clothes, accessories, and makeup can enhance, true beauty is impossible to hide. Raquel Welch, as example, was just as stunning as a filthy, sweating cave-woman in her early movie, One Million B.C. as she was in any of her later roles. The lingering glances of other males there proved he wasn't alone in his assessment. He watched her in awe, her head cocked as she read book spines, her hip testing the confines of her jeans, the jut of her breasts still visible beneath the billowy sweatshirt, forcing his mind to imagine each contour in finer detail.

She was the complete package, the kind of woman men covet. The kind they would kill for.

Paul's thoughts drifted from the assigned task to the question of how best to position himself for conquest of Monica Westfield. The revelation that she was single improved the odds. His stock was growing exponentially. They were both single, both pretty. She was accustomed to a standard of living that within days or weeks he could likely meet; and, as a woman, she had needs neglected until he rekindled her fires of passion. On second thought, this wasn't about positioning. He was already in place, having fallen there, magically. All he need do now was close.

Close the sale, Paul.

The term 'conquest' wasn't right either. Monica deserved better than that. It connoted vanquishing, one-night stands, and male bravado in smoky taverns about the newest notch in his belt. Their relationship would be much more than that. He could love her, share himself with her. He would give things up to please her. Stop the gambling? Okay! Sell the car? No problem. He would do anything to have and keep her. But how to make her feel the same?

Money?

There it was. The same obstacle Mason Brooks had to overcome. It was hard to hold it against the old guy. He used whatever resources were at his disposal. He couldn't have done it without the magic.

That same magic would soon be Paul's. The temptation to apply it here, to help win over Monica Westfield, would be strong, but its use was fraught with danger. Mason Brooks was a clever, intelligent man. He wielded his powers in methodical, scientific fashion. Paul simply wouldn't know how to use foresight to influence Monica, at least not initially, and probably never with Mason's creativity.

Monica's awareness would also handicap Paul. The magic had been used on her once, and would now be more difficult to disguise and deploy effectively.

The best argument against its use was the reaction it caused when she became aware of Mason's use of it on her. If she had any inkling that Paul was using the future to stalk her, he was through. She would hate him for eternity, just as she now did Mason.

This was a job he had to undertake himself. No gimmicks, no supernatural powers. Things were off to a good start. He simply needed to keep it honest and pure and let nature take its course. But how could he avoid taking advantage of obvious opportunities revealed to him? If reviews really did give him foreknowledge throughout the day, how could he not help but use what he knew to his advantage?

These were questions he couldn't answer. It was a matter best left to judgment. Call them as they come.

Mason, though, was another matter entirely. For all his brains, the man had weaknesses. There was the after-nine-o'clock blind spot, and while he might be adept at applying the magic, he'd yet to have it used on him. There was still the element of surprise. Mason was older and weaker too. Perhaps most important, Paul wanted nothing from him, other than learning how to make himself rich. After that, assuming he'd won over Monica and she was prepared to follow him, he was gone. Brooks was a fool. He foresaw his death, and got as close as he could to the source of the trouble.

Not Paul, no way would he make the same mistake. Once he got what he wanted, he'd be gone, agreement or no. Brooks would be on his own. It would be stupid to hang around and wait for their fates to mesh in some tragic end. With the Power he could see it happen in advance and avoid it. What better place for that than from halfway around the world? How could they possibly die together then, bonded together in some mysterious death dance as Mason would have him believe? Surely, a few thousand miles between them could rectify the dilemma. His first stop would be Las Vegas. He'd settle in for a week or two, pick up a few hundred grand there, then jump onto a cruise ship going who-the-hell-cares-where, as long as it had a casino aboard. Yeah, and check the passenger list ahead of time to make sure no coincidences put Brooks aboard the same boat.

He laughed at the thought of them on a sinking ship in the Bermuda Triangle. Maybe that would explain the bond.

After cleaning out the boat's casino, he and Monica could head for Monte Carlo and live in style in Europe, gambling, traveling, and making love nonstop. They could outrun Mason, never staying long in one place, with money never a concern and nothing to tie them down. Brooks wouldn't know where to look. At his age, they wouldn't have to run for long.

It was easy. Just convince Monica to go along.

She returned to the table and set down another book on card games opened to a chapter on blackjack.

"I hope that faraway look is you daydreaming about aces and face cards somewhere," she said, pulling out a chair across from him.

"Actually, I was thinking about you and me alone together on a desert island. I own it of course, and we're lying naked on the beach. I've had all the sand removed and replaced with coinage, mostly silver dollars, but enough dimes to make it comfortable."

Monica was about to sit, but held up. "You'd better take this seriously. Keep your nose in these books and don't waste your time, or you may not be around long enough to make your fantasies come true."

"Don't worry. I've got one-eyed jacks coming out of my rear."

"You'd better. You won't get many chances like this in life. I'm surprised Mason decided to do this for you. I don't see how a jaunt to Atlantic City fits into the research schedule."

"He said it would be better for both of us if I were independently wealthy, rather than him paying me for my services. If he can pull that off, I would agree. He also said something about picking up a few funds of his own."

Monica grunted and her eyes wandered. "Put your eyes on the page then," she said, tapping a finger in the open book lying in front of him. "I've seen Mason try this stunt a few times myself. It takes much concentration, and he doesn't always pull it off."

"Some encouraging words from you would help me stay more focused."

"I just gave you some. What else do you want?"

"Tell me that when I get some money and the knowledge to make more, that we're out of here together, you and me—Las Vegas, the Caribbean, Monte Carlo. Anywhere you want, just far away from Mason Brooks and this crazy problem of his."

"Be serious."

"I am serious." She had turned away and he reached across the table and took her hand. "Monica, there's nothing here for you. Give me a chance to give you a life, show you how a man should treat a woman. You deserve better than this."

She looked down at his hand on top of hers but made no attempt to remove it. "Paul, my life is very complicated and confusing right now. Don't ask me to make a decision like that."

"You're not saying no."

"Don't make the mistake of believing you can outrun fate. This tie you have with Mason has to be dealt with. You can't run off and hide and expect to cheat the gods. Stick with the research; it's your only hope."

"There's a little extra weapon I'm about to have that you're not considering. Distance is one thing, but controlling the future is another. I won't be cheating the gods—I'll be a god. I'll make the future what I want it to be. At least I could dodge Mason Brooks if I saw him coming."

Monica looked to be pondering that one.

"I'm not worried about it," he said. "Come with me."

Monica was waffling.

"You need time to think this out, but I'm sure that when you do, you'll see there's no reason to stay. You're not in danger. I don't think I will be, and if I'm not, then neither is Mason."

Paul became excited and put a finger in the air. "Maybe that's the key. Once I can see the future too, together we cancel any danger between us."

Monica was pulling her hand away.

"What is it, Monica? Do you still love Mason?"

"No," she said emphatically.

"Then there's something wrong with me."

"No." She sounded less emphatic, but added a convincing shake of the head.

"Give me a sign then. Let me know there's hope. Let me know you'll consider this, because once I get back from Atlantic City— assuming it's successful—I'm gone, with or without you. There would be no point in staying on and completing the research. Tell me there's a chance for us, and I'll glue my eyeballs to these books."

Monica hesitated.

Paul stared hard, then flashed a toothy grin, danced his eyebrows suggestively, and suavely ran his hand back through his hair.

"Maybe," Monica said. "That's the best I can do for now."

Chapter 17

Maybe Valium was what she needed, or Prozac. It was too bad she had neither. An anxiety attack, that's what she'd heard it called. Panic was a better description. Monica felt her nerves fraying. She pictured sinuous strands of fleshy fibers torn loose from her head and blowing wildly in the wind, sparks spewing forth like electric geysers.

All day she waged a silent war of indecision, with her sanity as the sole casualty. There was the marriage option, the loose plan she'd concocted the night before. Mason's odd decision to venture to Atlantic City and replenish his wealth was timely. If her plan was to make him pay, the more he had, the better. Marriage sounded logical.

Unfortunately, that morning Paul had further complicated matters with his own unique insights and proposals. Admittedly, he made her feel special in a way not felt for too long. There was an excitement. He made her feel good about herself. Clearly he was a more palatable choice than Mason. The thought of pushing back into the cockpit of his Corvette and driving into the sunset was tempting. He might be right about soon being able to generate his own wealth freely. That raised the question of whether distance and his own precognizant abilities could break the bond of death between him and Mason. That question was vast, and answered 'no' by the evidence she had seen.

Did it matter? If two infinitely rich men both loved her, did it matter with whom she went if financial independence was the ultimate goal? Should she care whether the bond held fast and took one or both to the grave? Of course.

Mason's actions were despicable, but not punishable by death. Paul was innocent of all but loose morals.

Having ruled out going it alone, Monica had to choose between the two men. If she followed her heart, it would lead her to Paul. Life could be good with him, with or without money. The proper thing to do was drop the vindictive plot to separate Mason and his money, and run off with Paul, settling for Mason's broken heart as justice served.

That brought her to the dilemma that had her head flaring with pain. She now shared Mason's faith that only the research could break the bond and save them both. If she openly chose Paul, he would run or Mason would throw him out. The research would end, the bond would live, and Paul or Mason would die. She would have encouraged the fatal steps. It would be the same as homicide.

If she openly chose Mason, it would crush Paul. Paul had threatened to leave after returning from Atlantic City. Only she could prevent that by warming to him and wiling him to stay.

Which should she do?

Decision-making was not her strong point, yet after a day tortured by these questions it became clear that she was a prisoner. She couldn't leave, nor could she choose one man over the other. That left only one option, choose both. This was a matter of life and death. All issues of morality, ethics, and personal desire aside, she must convince each man of her love for him, hide that fact from the other, and lead the research forward.

The logic was loose, the circumstances insane. Some crazy, invisible force was trying to kill one or both men, and she was the bond that could keep them alive and together, working on a solution. Only after the death-bond was broken could she consider her own feelings.

For success, she must appeal to each man's different needs and desires. With Paul, that was as simple and not-so-unpleasant as the occasional romp between the sheets. By his own admission he was no threat until after his return from Atlantic City. She could hold off his advances until then. With Mason, it required something more drastic to divert their relationship from its inevitable crash course. She would go with the proposal of marriage.

There it was. She was about to throw another dart, and this one felt heavy as a mortar shell.

She should have felt relief for reaching a tough decision—a mind made up, go or no go, right or wrong. That's what she wanted life boiled down to: decisions and consequences. Second-guessing had only led to self-doubt and inaction. There was no such relief, though. She sat in the study, staring transfixed into the glowing coals of the fireplace. The clock was ticking up to nine p.m. She was about to take rare, deliberate action. She was about to march up to Mason's room and break his edict against past-nine-p.m. interruptions and gamble three people's shaky future on a bizarre and distasteful ploy.

At five past nine she was still trying to convince herself that she was doing right. What if she failed? What if he rejected the offer? What if Paul found out about it? What would he think of that, the same day she had said 'maybe' to his offer?

At seven past nine the tears came, uncontrolled. She'd have to cancel. At eight past nine a rare wave of courage swept over her and she rose and ascended the staircase, still half-befuddled. Her last rational thought before turning the knob on Mason's door at the end of the hall was that the tears might serve her well.

She entered without knocking.

Mason stood on the near side of the bed, naked but for black socks and boxer shorts. His bedding was turned down and two dozen electrodes were attached to head, neck, upper torso, and a finger on each hand. Wires dangled off him and trailed into the thick underbrush of cords, cables and keyboards sheltering the bed he was about to climb into.

"For God's sakes," he said, obviously irritated by the intrusion.

Monica shut the door behind her and the tears gushed.

"What the hell's the matter?" Mason asked, almost shouting, and not out of concern for Monica.

She choked back the real tears enough to speak in broken sentences. "We need to talk."

"Can't it wait?"

"No. We need to talk now."

Mason lifted his hands and dropped them to his sides in frustration. Wires jangled. "Well, what the devil is your problem? You know what I've told you about disturbing me this late."

She fumbled with the strands of hair by her cheek. "I've been thinking about us."

Mason shut up.

"Things haven't been going right. Surely you've noticed it."

She waited for him to respond. Eventually he gestured, as if to say, 'Yeah, what's your point?' with head and hands.

"You've been treating me poorly. Things you say, little gestures. I know I'm right. I can feel this stuff. I'm a woman." The words were free-falling, spontaneous. "God knows I've been doing the same in return. I've said and done things I regret. We're pushing each other's buttons, growing farther apart. Something has to be done. We have to end this, for both our sakes."

A pained look came over Mason's face.

Monica saw the expression and immediately thought she was failing miserably. He was seeing through her like he had x-ray eyes. Maybe she'd been wrong and he still had some ESP sense this soon after nine. He seemed genuinely surprised by her visit and his expressions showed confusion, but maybe now he was receiving flashes and getting ahead of her. It was all falling apart. "Oh, Mason," she sobbed, dropping her face into her hands.

"Monica, don't do this," Mason said, his tone oddly different. "I'll have to admit, you're right about what's happening to us. I feel it too, but don't do this. We can work this out."

Monica popped her head up in surprise and watched Mason.

"You can't leave me now. I know I've been...preoccupied and

less of a gentleman than you deserve. I apologize for this. I've been under such strain. I know that if I can only get my hands around this research, we can work things out and rebuild our relationship. There's too much between us to throw away, and I don't mean to sound selfish, but I need you for my research. I can't do this alone. Please don't leave me now."

Monica stared in disbelief. "You silly old man. I'm not suggesting we break up. I'm asking you to marry me."

Mason's mouth formed a perfect 'O,' but no words came out.

Monica went on with her pitch. Mason stood stunned, listening, his growing smile hinting toward success.

"I don't know what to say," he said when she finished and stood awkwardly drying her eyes and blowing her nose.

"It's something you need to think about, I'm sure. Take time. I worried that with all your concerns, my timing was poor and motives selfish, but the thought of what lay ahead for us if I didn't do this convinced me."

"It's an interesting notion, I'll admit."

"Then there's hope. I'll leave it at that for tonight and let you get on with your recording."

Mason nodded, looking distant.

Monica stopped and faced the door before leaving. "There is one thing about this, Mason. I wouldn't mention it to Paul. I don't know if you've noticed, but I sense that he's...interested in me. If he were to find out that we're not already married, he may feel he has some right to pursue his interests before we do become married. Depending on how deep his interest is and how immature and unstable he is about rejection—as he might take it—telling him might not be the wise thing to do regarding the research. You never know. He might walk out."

Monica couldn't bring herself to look at the expression on Mason's face. She left the room without looking back.

Chapter 18

For fifty years Mason Brooks was not a morning person. A chronic over-sleeper and too often irritable, he required two cups of coffee to elevate him from his a.m. stupors. In the past two years his research had changed all that. The absolute need for consistent, timely, placid sleep ended a decades-long, six-cup-per-day coffee habit, and forced him to curb the runaway sweet tooth that fed his oversized belly, mood swings, headaches, and jittery nerves. Taming these vices surprised him. More than once before the research began he'd summoned all willpower, only to fail. Evidently, he lacked only proper motivation. Seeing the future provided all that he needed. Good diet became an integral part of his research. His mother would be proud.

While nutrition and rest played new roles, they were not what really drove Mason's metamorphosis into a bright-eyed riser, eager to face the day's challenges. Research was again at the wheel. Each day he woke filled with anticipation of what his review would reveal. Every day was Christmas morning with presents awaiting him under the tree. The feeling was absorbing, to know that within minutes he would again see the future, then throughout the day experience it and change it. The power was overwhelming, an intoxicating drug. Every morning was a new high. Even the threat of death added a special thrill.

He was addicted.

This morning was electric. He woke and began the ritual

rewinding of tapes and resetting of equipment necessary to end the nightly monitoring of his non-REM activity and begin the recall-stimulating replay. Before the review even began he knew this was a special day.

There were the developments with Monica. This had been a surprise—something he hadn't experienced for some time. He had felt surprise at realizing what was about to happen, but feeling the sharp stab of realization in present time had grown unfamiliar. Her message was as much a surprise in content as it was that he hadn't seen it coming, and it wasn't wholly unwelcome.

He didn't want to lose Monica. He wanted her for himself and needed her assistance in the research. Suddenly, just when he was convinced the end of their relationship was near, things were falling into place. Under the circumstances he had to question her motives, but her tears were real. If she had an ulterior motive, she gave the performance of a lifetime. What a tremendous, warm feeling it was to hear her proposal of marriage. He wanted to believe her. It was odd for her to say such a thing so shortly after being unfaithful to him, but perhaps it was that very act that precipitated the turnaround. It wasn't hard to imagine. A young woman tempted by the good looks, charm and excitement of a man more her age. Their own relationship was strained. Her life had become like that of a nun, with repetition, boredom, and celibacy. So she weakened, wandered, took the bait. Perhaps it wasn't what she expected. Maybe instead of falling in love with the rogue, she was having second thoughts, pangs of guilt, flashes of truth on what she was giving up. After all, Paul Fontana could hardly be considered marrying material, especially in comparison to himself. Maybe she has scruples. Maybe she's only human.

She failed the test, but learned the lesson.

Would he take her back now that she was used, spoiled, tainted by the hands of a lesser man? Did he want her? Oh, yes.

She was worth it, no matter what she had done. It didn't matter how either of them felt. He could hardly fault her for the purity of her feelings when his feelings and needs were less than noble too. What he wanted was them together. He wanted her to be his, period. Call it love, need, lust, possessiveness. Call it whatever. He didn't have much respect for her, but couldn't stand the thought of her leaving him and going with another man. If marriage was what it took to prevent that, then it was something worth considering. The beauty of marriage was that it wasn't something that had to happen immediately. He could stall, run it out a few months, try the notion on for size before signing the papers. If greed was her true goal, did that really matter either? If she treated him right, so what if she got rich from it. So what if they split and she got half? There was more where that came from.

This new turn of events with Monica only added to the urgency of resolving the crisis with Paul. 'Interests,' bloody hell. Monica's choice of words was clever, but she was hiding much more than she showed, he was sure. Plenty had gone on in the apartment that night. She wanted that kept secret, but more too. She wanted her proposal to Mason kept from Paul. What game was she playing? It was the old game of Play Both Ends Against the Middle, he guessed. This thing had to be fixed, and soon. While he might live with what Monica had done, his feelings toward Paul were another matter. He hated the man, and the relationship was going downhill from there.

Every minute this man was in their home was another minute of temptation for Monica, another straw on the back of their strained relationship. To preserve any hope of a successful marriage, Paul had to be removed from the picture.

Mason also gave thought to the fact that Paul, too, was rapidly acquiring the same ability to foresee the future. It was difficult to predict what this meant, but there were several interesting possibilities. Not all had pleasant repercussions for Mason.

A nagging question was popping up more often, and was again at the forefront. Mason had discovered that non-REM dreams reveal the next day's future, and that future can be manipulated.

The possibilities were seemingly infinite, but in the end, only one future could physically play out. If two people with intertwined existence both share this powerful ability to change the future, but don't share the same agenda, which future becomes reality? Who wins?

This question had growing importance to the issue of the bond between him and Paul. Soon he would lose the ability to control all aspects of his research of Paul and their daily lives. Paul would see things that Mason did before they were done and make changes of his own if he wished. This would send his scientific research program helter-skelter.

Worse yet, Mason theorized that two non-REM-enlightened individuals might wage a battle over manipulation of a shared future. Only one could win, the mentally strong, the essence of Darwinianism. What were the criteria for mental strength here, though? Intelligence? Quick wit? Memory? Creativity? Physical strength? Age? Life experience? There was no telling yet.

Therefore, fast action was essential. In the days ahead, Paul would likely begin to experience the same death dreams that plagued Mason. He would learn to avoid his death just as Mason had. That was not all he would learn to do. He could not be trusted to control his thoughts and actions if the bond of death seemed too imminent and unbreakable.

Mason flipped switches, settling back into the bed and feeling the vibrations and sounds of the replay flow through him. He wondered whether the subject he'd immersed himself in the previous day had the desired effect. There was a loose plan he had set in motion. The results of last night's non-REM dreams would reveal whether he would go with it.

If nothing worked out as he hoped, he was confident he would at least enjoy a successful day gambling in Atlantic City.

He could always use more money.

Chapter 19

If Paul's REM dreams were an indicator, his non-REM dreams wouldn't contain the knowledge needed to win in Atlantic City later in the day. Specific details of the REM dreams had slipped from memory now. What lingered were recollections of a restless night of bizarre dreams filled with vivid images of complicated love triangles, sex, violence, and odd snippets of conversation with his long-deceased mother.

He remained unusually silent earlier as Monica made the conversion of equipment from record to replay. She wasn't talkative either, which bothered him. He lay in bed, spinning his bracelet around his wrist, watching the woman he was falling in love with tend to him while she did her best to avoid him. She was a complete mystery.

Now she was back an hour later to terminate the review and free him from the electrodes. This, too, she did with the indifferent, methodical air of a career nurse retrieving a breakfast tray from another nameless patient.

Paul's third review since the first sign of success ended with the same lack of revelation and fanfare as the others; but Mason had progressed to the point that he 'saw' part of the day ahead during his review—actually recalling bits and scenes from his non-REM dream of the future—in addition to later having other parts revealed sporadically. Paul was not to that point yet. The hour passed as the others had, boring hums and vibrations revealing nothing. A waste of daylight.

Mason, however, also claimed another result of his reviews: a 'general sense' of what the day had in store for him, an overall flavor. Would it be a good day or bad, with significant events or not? He claimed to feel this after review, that paying it heed throughout the day doubled the frequency of visions.

Paul didn't know if his mood was such a result. That could be confirmed only by the reality of the day ahead, but there was a mood.

The jumble of emotions he woke to after dreaming in REM evolved over the hour-long review into a sense of dread, a fore-boding that descended like a thick, cold fog off an English moor, as if a werewolf bit him in the night, the moon was full, and his life was about to change forever.

He found himself absent-mindedly turning his bracelet again, so much now that the hair on his wrist was wearing off and the skin was red and sore. He flicked his wrist over and unlatched the bracelet. Clutching it in one hand, he took hold of Monica's arm with his other as she stood nearby, resetting a toggle switch.

"Don't, Paul," she said, reacting quickly and trying to pull away. "Mason could come in at any moment. He's very anxious to get at your results now that you're starting to make progress."

Paul held her firmly.

"There's no time for this," she insisted. "You promised to be a good boy. Don't let me down now."

Paul's gaze had been fixed on nothing, aiming past the end of the bed and trailing into the twilight zone. He turned his head and looked at her now, deep into her green pupils. He held out his clenched fist to her.

"Here. I want you to have this."

Her gaze went from his eyes to his hand, and back again. When it was clear that he wasn't going to let go of whatever it was he was holding until she accepted it, she offered an open palm. Paul dropped the bracelet into her hand and let go of her arm.

"What are you doing?" she asked. "I can't accept this."

"I insist."

She kneaded the solid eighteen-carat gold rope with her fingers and measured its heft in her open palm.

"I can't take this. Your mother gave it to you."

He pushed her hand away.

She looked at him closely and brought the chain up to her face, rubbing the etching between thumb and forefinger. She studied the inscription again.

Love is a bond stronger than life itself. My eternal love, Mother.

"I thought you said you've never taken this off before."

"Basically true."

"Uh huh," she said with a suspicious smile. "How many women have you pulled this trick on?"

That hurt. He was as sincere as he'd ever been. She didn't trust him. He shrugged it off.

"Never before, Monica. You're the only one."

She settled onto one hip and studied him more closely.

"What's with you? What's this about?"

Paul had the strangest feeling. He thought for a moment he was going to cry. He had words to say, but had to hold back until he got a grip on himself. Short sentences helped until he composed himself.

"Something's wrong."

"With what?"

"Me."

"What are you talking about?"

"I don't know."

She put her hands up. "You have to help me out here, Paul. Mason sees all. I don't."

"I've got a bad feeling."

Her face twitched, and her expression went serious. "A dream?"

"No. I didn't see anything. It's just a feeling. Something isn't right. I don't know."

Monica thought for a minute.

"It could be anything," she said. "Get some coffee. It'll go away."

He shrugged and sat up.

She held out the bracelet to him again.

He put up both hands in protest. "No. I want you to keep it. I insist."

"Paul, this has special meaning to you. Don't demean it or me with some foolish gesture."

"It does have special meaning to me. My dying mother gave it to me as a symbol of her love. I've carried it with me my whole life. Now I want to share its message with you."

"Why the big melodrama?"

"I feel something, something...evil. I can't explain why, but I'm scared. I feel like I'm in danger, like maybe I won't be coming back from Atlantic City tonight. It makes no sense and I don't understand it, but there's one thing that I am beginning to understand. I've got a feeling like I've never had before. I think I'm in love with you. I'm a big boy, Monica, and I see that you're not quite at the same point with me, although I hope you get there. Under other circumstances I might move slower and try not to scare you off, only I don't know if I have the time. No matter how you feel about me, I want this to be with you." He closed her hand over the bracelet.

She shut her eyes and sighed. "But it's from your mother."

"Let's put it this way, if I come back we can talk about me keeping it. If not, then I left it with the right person. It's my choice."

She shook her head and slowly broke a smile. Bending over him, she kissed him warmly on the lips, then brought the bracelet up and kissed that too.

That was the first overt move she had made toward him, other than a flirt, since meeting. He closed his eyes to fight back the illogical tears that seemed determined to wet his face after decades of dormancy. Damn them. He kept the eyes shut until after she was gone. She left quietly, slowly closing the door behind her as if he were sleeping.

What's happening? That wasn't the Paul Fontana of old, not the Man Behind the Wall, not the macho heartbreaker whose code of dating ethics was 'use the one you're with.' Where did this sensitive side come from? Was this love? Was all this because of Monica, or was it the dreams? Was there something out there to fear? Had he had one of Mason's ominous dreams? What good was it if he were unable to see it clearly, only sensing its vague threat?

Do you run or hide?

He flushed with emotion, and suddenly was crying. Fear poured down on him like cold rain, a fear that overwhelms, that lurks beneath a child's bed. Fear had chased him for a lifetime. In the first years after the death of his mother it caught him often and tortured him. As he grew, he learned to dodge it. That lessened the pain of being left alone in a cold world. He resolved that nothing would ever hurt him again. Not the fear. The wall went up, the gold chain barricaded the gate, and his dead mother became gatekeeper. He had felt a chink in the wall on that first visit to the Brooks' a few days ago as Mason explained his dilemma. Now a siege had breached the wall and the fear was overrunning him. There, within the inner walls, was a person who could hurt him. Monica. She had found a way past the defenses, past the gold gate, past the gatekeeper.

Now the golden gate was gone, in the hands of the person who could hurt him. Mother was gone too.

He was alone again.

He wiped his tears, embarrassed even in solitude.

Get hold of yourself, Fontana. Things aren't that bad. She kissed you. That's a good thing, and don't forget, today you become rich. Maybe there is a threat, maybe not. All you can do is go cautiously, use common sense. Use your deja vu to evade whatever it is, if you get any. Do what Mason says. Pay attention to the 'general sense.' Let it heighten your foresight.

Ironically, if the threat was from one of Mason's death-dreams, pitting Mason and Paul against the Grim Reaper, the safest place, he thought, was next to Mason, since his advanced ability to foresee and forestall the future could save them both.

This is crazy, he thought. Put miles between you and Mason and you must be safe; stay close and you must be safe. One must be wrong. Logically it would be the 'close' one. On another day, distance would be his choice, but today was payday. He couldn't pass on this opportunity in Atlantic City.

Then there was the gun.

He rarely visited Atlantic City without his gun. Only when he flew and there was no way past the airport metal detectors. He had taken to driving down simply for the added protection of a concealed weapon. There were too many unpaid debts, jealous men, and scorned women there. That's why Mason's choice of driving down was palatable. He first balked at the notion because a four-hour drive one way with Professor DullMouth sounded as fun as a trip to the proctologist, but this way the gun could go. Obviously, Mason was leery about flying with him out of fear that they would drop from the sky together, that despite his abilities he couldn't prevent disaster once airborne. In a car, Mason would have some semblance of control.

Following the same logic, Paul wanted to be as far away as possible from his gun this trip. It felt more like danger than protection today. He would leave it safe, right where he'd hidden it behind the dresser drawer in his room.

Paste yourself to the man who can save you, and avoid guns and pointy objects. Reduce the risks. Improve the odds.

One day, one trip, that was all it would take. The wall may be down and the gun at home, but the eyes and ears would be open. Get the money, a set of these gizmos for the future—maybe the woman too. Then we're out of here.

Chapter 20

When Monica wished the two gamblers good luck that morning, she could see that Paul was still disturbed. She tried to keep the mood cheery and upbeat despite him. If Mason noticed Paul's distant look, he made no indication. She doubted that Paul relayed his concerns to Mason. She said nothing to him either. Since first hearing of their plan to visit Atlantic City, the idea had grown on her. Every hour, it seemed, a new angle occurred to her, another reason the trip would end in positive result. She wasn't about to sound an alarm that might cause them to cancel.

Their trip was a breather for her, a day of freedom from both men, a time for reflection and relaxation. The men rose early and drove off shortly after six a.m., planning to fit in six or seven hours of blackjack before returning in time for Mason's nine p.m. curfew. She was to stay home near the phone and make no calls that would tie it up in case he needed her for something.

She was glad they were gone. The Good Wife was a tough act. She couldn't stomach another minute with Mason. Paul could not be trusted to say or do the right thing in front of Mason, and his hands were incorrigible, constantly finding their way onto her body and roaming free. That wasn't necessarily a bad thing, but his timing was atrocious.

Mason would, of course, win money. There was nothing wrong with that. Paul's winnings weren't guaranteed, but his odds were better than the typical casino patron. With her fate seemingly woven into both their lives, the more money each had, the more secure her future appeared.

There was a worry with the trip, though. Logically, with Paul a threat to Mason's life, the more time they spent together, the more inevitable the outcome. She and Mason also held the conviction that only research of Paul's dreams held the cure, something only Mason could do. Ironically, their proximity was their only hope. What their trip had to do with research was the question that plagued her. It seemed frivolous and risky.

After bidding them farewell and watching the car disappear up the street, she repaired to the kitchen for cappuccino, a stimulant she felt her nerves could now handle as she enjoyed a stress-free day alone. Wrong choice. Sitting on a stool at the island counter, sipping away and counting her blessings, a few new angles began to occur to her. That's when the problem began. Caffeine or no, her hands began to shake.

A persistent question really tugged at her now. Why was Mason going to Atlantic City? Why was he teaching Paul his tricks? On the surface it was unnecessary. They had an equitable deal. Paul was apparently satisfied. Why do this? To prove it could be done? No good. As a gesture of goodwill? Hardly. It didn't fit into the research puzzle. It was a mystery.

A notion began to form, though.

Perhaps Mason had discovered something. Maybe there was no cure, no way to break the bond. Maybe the answer was distance between them. Maybe he was enriching Paul purposely, providing him with the means to leave the country and lead a comfortable life beyond fate's reach.

Or...he somehow knew what took place in Paul's apartment. To buy him off, he was going to teach Paul his gambling tricks, worried that Paul threatened their possible marriage.

None of these sounded quite right. Something was going on. Something didn't fit. There was a reason, and if she had to guess, it had to do with Mason wanting Paul out of the house and out of his life for good. Making him rich played into that somehow.

That led to another question. What would Mason do to Monica if he knew the truth about her? She tried to imagine herself inside his conniving mind. She squinted and thought hard. If I were Mason, I'd...write her out of the will.

Her heart thumped when she thought it. She set down her china cup and dashed through the swinging door. Skidding dangerously on the braided, oval rug at the base of the staircase, she turned and charged up to Mason's room three steps at a time. Jogging the hall to his room, she threw open the door and went straight to the roll-top, heaving it up without regard to its fragile, antique condition. She knew right where to look; Mason had repeated his instructions often. There it was. VOID.

It was splashed across the face of the document, unmistakably Mason's handwriting, nonerasable ink—not rewritten, simply voided, an unbelievable development. She shuffled through each page. They were all the same. He was thorough.

She slumped into the swivel chair, banging an elbow on the wooden armrest. She was hyperventilating. The world was coming to an end.

Mason either knew about her infidelity or he'd seen right through her pitiful attempt to outwit him and marry his money. It didn't matter which. She was finished, sure to be living out of a cardboard box in front of some sleazy uptown mall by Christmas.

Something she was sitting on poked uncomfortably into her rear. She reached into the back pocket of her jeans and pulled out Paul's bracelet, only now remembering she had tucked it there earlier. Dumb. What if Mason had seen the lump in her pocket or brushed it with his hand when pecking her goodbye? What if he'd asked about it? It was careless, but hardly mattered now.

She rubbed it, staring through it, focused on nothing. It was odd that Paul would give her this; a beautiful gesture, one that flattered and left her musing on life with the attractive and romantic Paul Fontana after the bond was broken. But while love was the message he wanted sent, fear had prompted him to part with it. What kind of fear makes a man part with such a treasure, mortal fear? Were the reviews having their effect? What was it he'd seen, or in this case, felt?

She couldn't be sure, but it was likely death due to the bond. Had he finally sensed one of the shared dreams that Mason theorized he may unwittingly experience in non-REM? Mason could see these events and prevent them. Paul could not. How would a man react to such a fear, a creeping invisible certainty, reversible only by those with the foresight and nerve to effect change?

Paul's foresight may not yet be twenty-twenty, but he was a man of nerve, not one to stand idly by and let fate as he knows it flatten him like so much roadkill on the highway of time. He would act, but how?

The gun.

The thought of it was a muzzle flash. God, she thought. That's why he gave me this thing. He's going to kill Mason.

He must have seen that as the only way out. Mason stood between them, and between Paul and old age. Either he wasn't sure he'd live through the job, or expected to spend his life in prison, or thought he'd no longer be worthy of carrying the bracelet, a symbol of love and hope. That's why he passed it on to her. That's what this was about. It explained his bizarre mood and why he agreed to a trip that he sensed had his death written all over it. It did more than explain, it fulfilled the bond's charter.

With Mason's death goes all hope. She checked the will again. His instruction to void it was dated. She couldn't think straight, but it wasn't today's date, or yesterday's. What had he been thinking at the time? It couldn't have been the marriage proposal, could it? No, too early for that. He couldn't have known about that yet. She didn't know about it then. Maybe he'd acted impulsively in a fit of anger, perhaps having learned about Paul and her. His positive reaction the previous night to the topic of marriage seemed sincere. It had to be. He wasn't faking his surprise. He hadn't had time to think it through, and didn't get back to reversing this will. Maybe wouldn't until he was more sure of the situation. As long as Mason was alive there was hope of correcting the will and salvaging a future for herself.

Despite Mason's crimes against her, the thought of Paul shooting him in cold blood made her shudder and her stomach flop. She stood to lose more than money and the opportunity to get even with Mason. She'd lose Paul, too. The hot-blooded fool had no chance of getting away with it. With her fists tightly balled and pressed to her forehead, she finally admitted what had been a fleeting thought, ratified by his sincerity the night before, and now thrust upon her by the prospect of losing him forever. She loved the man. Not only would his incarceration end their future together, if he murdered, she could never face him again.

Please, don't do this, Paul.

She stood and repocketed the bracelet. Maybe she was wrong. Maybe the gun was still resting there, down the hall and behind the drawer. That wouldn't make sense, and seemed unlikely. Why would Paul sneak it into the house, only to leave it when he presumably needed it most? There was only one way to find out.

It was so simple. Walk the thirty feet, open a door, pull out a drawer, peek into the darkness, confirm what you already know. No surprise, no big deal. Why was it so hard to do?

She walked slowly, stopping twice, trying to think of any obvious fact she had missed, anything that would eliminate the necessity of doing it. She entered Paul's room and faced the bureau, seeing herself in the mirror on top. She was crying and hadn't noticed. The gun scared her. It was an instrument of bewitching beauty and intrigue, so solid, heavy, cold and final. She feared to look because of what its absence would represent. It was as if the gore it may have already wrought was piled behind that drawer, a bloody, pulpy mess.

What unthinkable acts were people capable of? What was she capable of with such a tool in her hand?

Cautiously, she pulled the drawer out and set it on the dresser top. Kneeling down, she held her breath and peered into the dark cavity.

The gun was gone.

Chapter 21

"Are you feeling better?" Mason asked as he drove. "You looked a bit ragged there earlier. The dealership doesn't normally open at six a.m., does it?"

Not bothering to answer, Paul yawned and stretched as best he could in the car's front seat, waking from a two-hour nap. He wasn't an early riser, yet this morning they managed to review, shower, dress, and grab coffee for the road—all before the sun rose. The first half-hour on the road passed in silence. They reached the interstate before rush-hour and cruised smoothly among the semis and long-distance commuters, the BMW handling the seventy-five-mile-per-hour pace with no hint of excess noise or vibration. Thankfully, Paul had drifted off to sleep quickly, avoiding another of Mason's uplifting lectures on the likes of Positron Emission Topography, frontal lobe metabolism, nuerophysicology, and the host of other boring topics he'd bombarded Paul with over the past few days.

He felt better now. Gone was the oppressive gloom. In its place was a wary calm.

"Where are we?" he asked, wiping his eyes and rubbernecking a peek at the speedometer. He noticed that Brooks, three hours into their drive, still wore the gray leather driving gloves he'd worn as they left the house, an eccentricity that perfectly fit Paul's image of the man.

"Another seventy minutes, I'd say."

Damn. That was an eternity when receiving personal tutoring from Mister Science Project himself. The key to maintaining sanity from here on was in controlling the conversation, not necessarily doing the talking, just steering it out of the lab.

"Why take Monica's car?" he asked, not caring in the least.

"Nothing sinister, I assure you. I'm afraid that for all my wealth, I've never understood the American obsession with the automobile. A wonderful invention, but how some can coddle and coo over a mindless tangle of sheet metal and wire, I cannot fathom. Cars serve a singular purpose, to transport objects from one location to another. In my opinion, that function, like all others, should be done as efficiently and cost effectively as possible. That rules out pinstriped bug shields and leather bumper bras. My vehicle is a Mercedes, a technological marvel. Unfortunately, its twelve years and protracted state of disrepair make it unsuitable for a long venture such as ours. It's too unreliable, though perfectly dependable for what little travel I do between home and the university. Monica's tastes are another matter, however. Comfort and style are paramount. Basic utility is secondary. Although I must say," he said, tapping the dash, "this vehicle is extraordinarily adequate."

Sorry he asked, Paul made small, unnoticeable faces with his mouth, mimicking Mason. Mason's attitude toward cars belittled Paul's career as car salesman. "You can keep them both as far as I'm concerned. They're both junk."

Mason turned and looked puzzled. "How's that?"

"Foreign cars are butt-ugly and overpriced. This one's typical, like riding a pillow. You can't hear the engine or feel the road. How are you supposed to know when something is wrong? I've never owned anything but an American car, and never will."

Mason stole two quick glances at him as if checking to see if he were serious, then opened his mouth to speak.

Paul threw up a hand and cut him short. "Wait," he said, pointing at him, "I know what you were going to say. 'Quite.' You were going to say 'quite,' weren't you?"

"Yes I was, by Jove."

Instantly, Paul's outlook on the day turned positive.

"This is momentous," Mason said. "You realize what this means, don't you? Thus far you've experienced deja vu too late to act on it, but for the first time, you saw far enough ahead to use the knowledge. Now you can change the future. Don't you see? I was indeed about to say 'quite,' a meaningless figure of speech left over from my days abroad. I'm afraid I use it too often, and completely unwittingly, but since you stopped me, I didn't say it as I intended. The future changed infinitesimally. In a trivial way, the universe will never be the same. As your power grows, so will your impact on the course of your own destiny."

"Like becoming filthy stinking rich."

Both pointed a finger at each other and said 'quite' simultaneously with enormous smiles on their faces.

Five more miles passed before Paul spoke again. He spent the time trying to comprehend what it all meant. It was odd, he thought. There sat Mason, two years ahead in applying the Power and two thousand years of evolution ahead in understanding it, yet his silence was telling too. Was that what this was like? A never-ending quest for comprehension? An ever-expanding pile of knowledge with only a spade of understanding to move it?

Perhaps, but he'd settle for an ever-expanding pile of money.

"I don't 'feel' anything about blackjack yet," he said. "Will I see what move I should make right before I place my bets?"

"If you 'see' anything, that's what will happen, but don't expect much of it. Remember to play your hunches. Don't second-guess yourself. Don't expect to win all hands, you won't."

"How am I supposed to know how to bet if I don't see it in advance? The bet has to be placed beforehand, you know."

"Bet conservatively and consistently. It's not the big one-hand kill you're looking for, it's a tipping of the odds, a preponderance of small wins that snowball into a tidy accumulation."

Paul sat sideways, staring at Mason, absorbing the instructions fully. This wasn't sounding as surefire and exciting as he'd hoped. He wanted to sweep through the casinos like a firestorm, bagging a lifetime's wealth in one session.

"Look, Paul, don't let greed distract you. You must clear your mind and let your dreams work for you. Remember, this trip isn't intended to make you independently wealthy. You're here to learn to do that later, on your own. In fact, I think I can tell you this, I've prepared for today myself and intend to win some too, and from what I've seen, you go most of the day without winning. Might even lose some."

Paul's face fell.

"But, you have a big surprise coming later in the day. I've seen that."

"What is it?"

"I can't tell you that now. If I did, it would change the future so much that it may never happen for you. Do you understand this?"

Paul nodded vaguely.

"You must learn that when you foresee a favorable event, you need to be extremely cautious about what you say or do up to that point. The future is very fragile. The dreams can help you avoid the negative, but if you're not careful, they can just as easily alter the positive."

For Paul, the morning's fears were a distant memory. The day now passed with electric anticipation. Strangely, he also now respected Mason on some level. He was heading to Atlantic City, his own domain, yet he looked to Mason for guidance and protection. He laughed inwardly at the thought of them under other circumstances taking their unlikely friendship to a yuppie uptown cocktail party. The suave, with-it, seductive Paul, with Mason in tow, the brilliant old scientist with spiked gray hair, black lab glasses and plastic pocket protector. Hi, everyone. This is my friend, Mason. Tell them about it, Mason. Tell them how it is.

You and me could party, pal.

Mason took an exit ramp off the freeway, thirty miles from Atlantic City. "We need gas," he said, turning left, crossing the overpass, and driving past two perfectly good stations.

"What's wrong with one of those?" Paul asked, pointing with a thumb over his shoulder.

"I don't have a credit card for those brands," he said, fumbling with his left hand in the inside breast pocket of his sport coat.

They traveled another few hundred yards down the road and pulled into a grubbier, less popular-looking station. Mason rolled up to the pump farthest out and lowered his power window. Dangling his left arm out the window and down the side of the car, he crept past the pumps without coming to a complete stop. Doing so, he glanced suspiciously at the building and over his shoulder and out each window of the car as if worried someone was watching. He drove on then, back onto the road, closed his window, and headed back to the freeway.

"What's that about?" Paul asked.

"I must have forgotten that credit card at home. We'll catch another station at the next exit."

Paul shook his head. Evolution, hell. A lifetime of experience and education, the ultimate prophet, he knows all, sees all, yet under it all he's still the absent-minded professor who can't remember his wallet.

Will wonders never cease?

Chapter 22

Wanting to be seen with Paul as little as possible, Mason had moved to another blackjack table long ago. The cards were falling nicely for him and he was winning one fifty-dollar hand after another. The value of his chips multiplied well into the thousands. He knew this would happen, of course, yet curiously never tired of the process.

Paul, though, was still stuck at a ten-dollar table, not enjoying the same success.

They had started the day's gambling together. Paul was talkative and jovial then, high on the prospect of winning big. When his losses outnumbered his gains in the first hour, he was unfazed. When they continued to mount by noon, however, his mood changed. He became irritable and vocal, a spectacle of pouting and foot-stomping.

On their breaks, Mason reminded Paul of his premonition of early failure and late success. That pacified Paul for a time, but when losses bankrupted him by mid-afternoon he was beside himself. Mason pulled him aside and continued to assuage him, bankrolling him with some of his own chips.

"I haven't 'seen' a single hand yet, Brooks," Paul said, "and the only 'feeling' I'm getting is that this whole thing is a pile of crap. It's not working."

"But it is, Paul. This is exactly what I've seen. Stick with it. You must return to the table and press on. Your luck is about to turn. I believe you will have a clear preview of at least one hand. That alone will demonstrate the truth and the power of what I offer you. And don't forget, my young friend, you have a surprise yet to come."

Paul sighed in exasperation. "What surprise?"

"Patience, dear boy, patience."

Paul returned to his table and gambled on. Mason was on edge, pacing the carpeted rows of slot machines, purchasing a sandwich and soda, and visiting the restroom before returning to his own table for further gains. He checked his watch often as the time neared four p.m., and he continually peered over his left shoulder at Paul's back across the room, both knowing and wondering how he was progressing.

At quarter past four Mason heard Paul hooting in triumph from across the room. He turned and looked, as had most of the casino's patrons. Paul was standing and pumping his arm in the air, making a scene. A smattering of applause rose from the room as other gamblers cheered on the nameless winner who represented the chance that they, too, could at any moment win big. No doubt the dealer and patrons sharing Paul's table were confused on why a man with steady losses would suddenly become so exuberant over a single ten-dollar win. They had no way of knowing what Mason knew, that Paul didn't just win the hand, he'd known about the win before the cards even came down.

Mason played another hand, excused himself from the table, and made his way to the cashier's window, converting all his chips to as many hundred dollar bills as possible. Nonchalantly roaming toward Paul's table, he circled it, standing behind the dealer, facing Paul. When he made eye contact with Paul he winked and signaled with his head for him to follow. Paul grabbed his chips and met Mason across the room near a vacant bank of video poker machines.

"What gives, man?" he said, with an inquisitive look. "I was just starting to win. You were right. I saw a hand just like you said. This is going to work."

"I need to explain something to you," Mason said, putting his hand on Paul's shoulder and keeping his voice down.

"Another pep talk?"

"Trust me, this is important," Mason said. "You need to behave discreetly to have any meaningful success, at least in casinos. There are, of course, other ways to profit from your new ability, but I assume that games of chance are your bailiwick, so understand that people who run casinos watch for people like you, particularly in blackjack. They don't like to lose, at least not consistently. The occasional winner is important to keep the suckers streaming in, but casinos ban card-counters and scam-artists for life. This happens frequently. Once you're known, the word will spread and your gambling days are through."

"I know all that," Paul said, "but I'm not card counting or scamming."

"Ah, but they don't know that. It won't matter how you come by your winnings. If you beat the odds too consistently, they have no alternative but to believe that you have a system, which of course you do. They don't have to understand how you do it to ban you."

Paul shrugged.

"That's why the key to success is discretion. Stay low key. Do not attract attention to yourself. Do not stay long in one casino. Move along. Dress differently each time, conservatively. Blend in. Most important, don't be greedy. Never sit at anything higher than a hundred-dollar-bet table, and always bet the minimum. Make your wealth incrementally, a bit here, a bit there. Lose enough to make it look real. Your exuberance back there was understandable, but it must never happen again. Do you understand this?"

"It makes sense."

"Fine then. You have enough time for a few more hands, then we'll have to return home," Mason said.

"What about this damn surprise? If I've got another vision coming, shouldn't I move to a higher-stakes table and make it worthwhile?"

Mason fought back the urge to crack a wry smile. Paul was hooked.

"No, stay where you were," he said. "I have to admit something. I don't know exactly what the surprise is, because apparently I don't see it happen. All I know is that when we ride home tonight, you're wearing a four-hour smile. Something very good will happen to you in the next half-hour, but you never do tell me what it is."

Paul shrugged with open palms in a questioning gesture.

"Trust me, Paul. Have I been wrong yet?"

"You're the man, Mason."

Paul headed back to his table with a pocketful of chips, smiling all the way. Mason went in the direction of the restrooms near the cashier's window, but once out of Paul's view, bypassed them and took a side exit leading into the hotel. Passing down a long hallway he turned right and exited the building through a locked side door intended to restrict entry to all but hotel guests with passkeys.

Satisfied he'd made an inconspicuous exit and that he and Paul had not been seen leaving together, he turned and aimed for the casino's main entrance along the Boardwalk. After donning his gloves and standing in the cold for a minute just outside the door, Mason spotted a lone patron walking up the Boardwalk from the south, heading for Bally's Park Place. Mason pulled an envelope from his inside jacket pocket and approached the middle-aged man as he reached for the door.

"Pardon me, sir, but a very attractive young lady just handed me this and asked that I deliver it inside, but I'm afraid I'm in a bit of a hurry and I'm on my way out. Would it be too much of an imposition to ask that you deliver it for her?" He thrust the letter into the other man's hand.

The stranger looked the envelope over. "What did she want you to do with it?"

"Very simple. Just drop it at the cashier's window and ask that

they page this person." He pointed at the name, Paul Fontana, typed on the envelope. "Apparently it's a message for him."
The man shrugged. "Sure."
Mason thanked the man and immediately walked off in the direction the stranger came from. He walked across the broad Boardwalk to the ocean side, looking down upon the beach below. It was empty of people as far as the eye could see.
The landmark Boardwalk was a wooden structure extending several miles along the shoreline. The walkway was a major tourist destination in Atlantic City. All twelve casinos opened onto it, and numerous shops, restaurants, and entertainment centers lined its side. Four large piers shot off the Boardwalk on a tangent toward the sea, their supporting pillars growing steadily taller as the shoreline fell away. Several hundred yards from Bally's Park Place, Mason turned onto the southernmost of these, the Ocean One Pier.
Ocean One Pier was an enormous edifice having nothing to do with allowing passengers access to oceangoing vessels. It was a prime example of Atlantic City's investment in the tourism trade. Virtually the entire surface of the pier was built up with restaurants and a collection of stores known as The Shops at Ocean One.
By now Mason was sure his envelope had been delivered as promised back at the casino and that Paul had been paged and was at that moment standing near the cashier's window reading the message. He could picture Paul's broad smile upon reading the cryptic letter, purportedly from Monica, stating her desperate need to see him and asking him to immediately meet her under Ocean One Pier. Paul, shocked that Monica would have followed them to Atlantic City for an urgent and private meeting with him would, of course, assume that this event was related to the 'big surprise' Mason had predicted, and that Monica had some kinky desire to make love in the cold sand beneath the Boardwalk or, better yet, wished to run off with him. After all, the letter was signed with a typewritten, "Love, Monica." Slipping away before

Mason could check out why Paul had been paged, he would rush off, eager to experience whatever it was that could keep him smiling for four hours.

The sun had disappeared behind the buildings to the west and the eastern horizon was dark and getting darker by the minute. A thirty-mile-per-hour wind was gusting in off the water, making the forty-five-degree temperature feel colder than it was. A pall of grey clouds hung in the sky as the result of a persistent low pressure area, and the salt air smelled of the coming winter. Late November wasn't Atlantic City's busy season. That and the gloomy weather emptied the Boardwalk of all but a few people using it to get from point A to point B, heads down into the wind, scurrying quickly, oblivious to the occasional passing stranger.

Mason held his jacket closed with one hand and tried to bury his head in the neck hole like a turtle in its shell. The leather driving gloves helped keep his fingers warm.

Going right, he descended a wooden staircase leading to the shore below. Staying beneath the massive pier overhead, he trudged through the sand and past the pillars toward the surf.

Ten feet from the surging tide he stopped and leaned against the last pillar on dry ground, waiting. Mason knew of Paul's familiarity with the city. Paul would follow the letter's brief directions successfully. Mason knew he was coming. He had already seen their meeting.

Five minutes passed. Then Mason heard a muffled voice shouting into the wind from behind. He turned and peered into the twilight beneath the pier, hiding himself from view behind his post. Again he heard the shouting, closer now. This time he recognized the voice. It was Paul, calling Monica's name.

Mason stood straight and moved as required to keep the pillar between them. Paul trotted up to within a dozen feet of the pillar and stopped.

"Monica!" he called again.

Mason stepped coolly from behind the pillar and spoke loudly to be heard over the wind and waves. "Monica won't be joining us here today, Paul."

Startled, Paul jumped back and grunted. "What's this?"

Mason turned his head and looked out at the ocean for a moment, pensive and silent. When he turned back, he lifted his right arm, which he had hidden behind him, and aimed the .38 caliber Smith & Wesson revolver he was holding directly at Paul's forehead.

Paul's eyes doubled in size and he stumbled back a step, withdrawing his hands from his pockets and suspending them in the air by his sides as if to draw pistols from an invisible set of holsters at his waist.

"I'm terribly sorry about the deception, Paul. It was I who wrote the note and had you paged. I was afraid that you might be too suspicious to follow me out here alone, streetwise as you are. I guessed that a nice note from Monica might lure you. I seem to have guessed correctly."

Paul's mouth hung open. He tried to speak, but no words came out.

Mason held the gun steady. "I'm sure you're wondering what this is about, Paul, so I'll try to explain. I'm afraid it's bad news. You see, I quickly realized after your astounding rate of progression with the reviews that I would soon lose all ability to protect myself from you. You could change the future too. Your deja vu in the car on the ride down here and your brief success at the blackjack table confirm this. My dreams have revealed the dichotomy before me. It seems that the bond between us cannot be broken. You would soon come to the same conclusion and act as I am now. It's only a question of who kills whom first. My advanced experience with the research gives me an edge over you, and I must take advantage of the element of surprise while it still exists. It may be cliché, Paul, but quite literally, this town ain't big enough for the both of us."

Paul took another tentative step back. "You can't do this."

"There's a mandate from a higher power that one of us must go, and I appear to be the one with the gun."

"That's my gun, isn't it?"

"Yes, it is, Paul. I'm sorry about that too, but if I didn't do this, you'd be pointing it at me tomorrow, or perhaps the day after. It's only a question of time."

Paul stole a quick glance to his side, searching for anyone on the beach there in the failing light who could help him. There was no one.

"You don't believe all this, Brooks," he said. "You can't really mean this. This isn't you."

"I'll tell you another thing, Paul. This is not an easy thing, certainly not something I've done before or even imagined myself doing, but the task is a fraction easier knowing that it must be done to you. There's no one that I'd rather have to do this to now."

Paul's hands rose slowly, without conscious effort, to a defensive position in front of his chest, palms open to Mason, fingers splayed, ready to deflect bullets if they came. At the last comment they tilted, like a confused dog cocking its head. "What did I do to you?"

"You didn't really think you could get away with it, did you?"

"We can forget the money. I'm sorry about putting the pinch on you."

"Your extortion was annoying, but I'm referring to you and my wife."

Paul wilted. He rubbed his face and repositioned his hands in the space before him as if they alone could contain the situation and buy him time.

Mason watched him squirm. This was dragging on a bit longer than planned, and the exhilaration surprised him. Paul was obviously in a desperate search for the right words, the ones that would talk him out of his deadly predicament.

"She's not your wife," he blurted.

"Fair game, eh? Did she tell you that before or after?"

"Brooks, we can work this out. I can leave the country. I'll send you money. I'll pay you back for everything. This doesn't have to happen. Please."

Mason waited. A thin smile formed on his face.

Then it happened.

The expression on Paul's face changed suddenly and completely. The color of his face drained to a light gray, and his hands fell to his side. "Oh, my god," he said staring through Mason and past the night.

Paul was now witness to the event about to happen.

Despite seeing the outcome, Paul lunged forward, betrayed by instinct. He grabbed desperately for Mason's gun hand, but his backward steps had left too wide a gap between them.

Mason knew what to expect, having dreamed it the night before. He deftly sidestepped Paul's charge, and spinning to flank as he passed, swung the gun and fired one shot at the side of the younger man's head.

Wind and waves muffled the sound. The bullet's impact threw Paul's head violently to the side where it slammed hard into the pillar that Mason had hidden behind earlier. His head bounced off and Paul crumpled to the ground like a man with no bones.

He gurgled for a moment and twitched spastically in the cold sand.

Chapter 23

The day went poorly for Monica. Neither television nor books could distract her from the matter at hand. She wavered between belief and skepticism. The situation was so entirely improbable, two men so inherently harmless. Repeatedly she convinced herself it was overreaction, only to recall the very real presence of the gun, the changed will, Paul's mood, the omnipresent bond. The circumstantial evidence was compelling.

She passed the hours in the study, near the phone, feet raised, her mind buried beneath a pile of unanswered questions. The day that she hoped would provide a respite from torment had become a silent, slow-motion hell of ticking seconds and pounding possibilities.

The age-old question haunting her for a lifetime droned in her ear like a mantra. What now, Monica Westfield? What now?

In the early panic that morning, after concluding that Paul would murder Mason, she'd reached for the phone, intent on stopping him before it was too late. The receiver went up and down several times as she decided whom to call and then decided against it.

Whom could she call? Who could help her? The two had not left an itinerary of casino stops. She had no idea which of the twelve they would visit. All, perhaps. They were down only for the day, and wouldn't rent a room. There was no way to contact them directly short of calling each casino and having them paged.

Whom would she ask for? Mason, to warn him, or Paul to talk him out of it? What proof did she have? What could she say to either of them? If she asked for Paul and succeeded in stopping him, it would look to Mason as though she had conspired with Paul. Mason would throw them both out, and dash all her hopes. If she spoke with Mason, he would know about it before she did so. What new convolutions would that add to the stew?

She could ask the police to intervene, but what crime would they be acting on? Intention of attempted murder? Conspiracy? What about evidence? Which of her activities would she have to reveal to Mason and the world to prove that? Anyway, the police don't work that way. They work reactively. Call us when there's a body, ma'am. What would they think of her call once the murder had taken place? How could she have known? What role had she played? She wouldn't be above suspicion at some level.

There was no one else to call. She was helpless, frozen, blinded in the headlights of manifest destiny.

She was envious of Mason's power to foresee the future and tinker with it to suit his desires, but she knew the truth, the veritable law of nature as it applied to Monica Westfield, planted like a seed by her father when she was but a sprout. She would have no clue how to use the power if it were hers. The future could do her no good. She couldn't make the decisions needed to alter it in her favor. Today was a classic example. With no doubt about Paul's intentions, and the repercussions, she sat on her hands, indecisive, a mapless traveler at the junction of life and death.

With no viable options left, she sat staring, catatonic, waiting for the phone to ring. Perhaps Mason would call to check in. What would she tell him? What if the police called? What if Paul called, asking her to run off with him? The most likely, it seemed, would be his return home to get her. What would she say? How would she act with her budding love then stopped cold? There was no prospect of their living happily ever after, not after murder. Did he expect to get away with it? He was not a bright man, but impulsive, spontaneous. There couldn't have been more than a few hours of forethought devoted to the task, not enough to out-wit the authorities and hide the trail of evidence leading to him. She was part of that trail. Would she side with him, knowing what she knew? Could she risk the chance of being named an accomplice? After all, she knew something he did not, a key section of the trail of evidence. The private investigator, Roger Wilkins. No one else in town knew any connection between Mason Brooks, Monica Westfield, and Paul Fontana. If Paul made a clear getaway from Atlantic City, he would return here believing he was free and clear, but what if the local paper ran a story on the murder of the local man in Atlantic City and the investigator read it? This was a man he investigated for. He knew about Paul and the gun. He knew nothing about motive, perhaps, but the need for his services alone was cause for suspicion. He would go to the police, and Paul would be through. She couldn't support Paul in such a case.

There was no future in a relationship with a convicted murderer, whatever his motive.

Chapter 24

The bloody wound on the side of Paul's head held Mason captivated for a time. The deed hadn't been as difficult as he feared. Now done, a sense of satisfaction not envisioned swept over him, a fulfillment, a burden lifted. The bond hadn't been broken after all, but dissolved, its directive accomplished.

He calmly pocketed the weapon and kneeled over the face-down body. Reaching into Paul's pants pocket, he withdrew a half-dozen poker chips and, pulling his head back by the hair, stuffed them up into the open mouth cavity. He removed Paul's wallet from his back pocket and slipped it into his own. In another pocket he found the note that lured Paul into the trap. He took that too. One more long look, then he made his way back up the stairs, off the pier, across the Boardwalk, and swiftly yet nonchalantly returned to the car. Three minutes later he was on the Atlantic City Expressway, heading northwest at a reasonable speed sure not to attract the attention of law enforcement. He exited north onto the Garden State Parkway and aimed for home.

Ten minutes passed, twenty, a half-hour, an hour. He waited for the flood of emotion, the pangs of guilt, the tears, the nausea, but there was none.

He'd just killed a man, and all he felt was the ease of it.

This was something to which he had given much thought. How would he react to his own deed? Could he live with the outcome? Where was his superego?

This development was fascinating and worthy of further research. Now free of the bond, he would devote it full attention. Not only did he tap the id itself, but, oddly, this apparently suppressed the superego as well. He didn't need to read a book to know that id-dominated personalities devoid of the remorse doled out by the superego were a problem for society. If this was the inevitable result of non-REM review, the world was better off without Paul Fontana. He couldn't be expected to reason through his altered intrapsychic mix with the same application of logic as Mason. In the right hands, a suppressed superego could be an effective tool, allowing one to make tough, logical choices without the hindrance of debilitating guilt. His necessary, premeditated murder of Paul Fontana was a perfect example, and if the newly rearranged id-superego ranking helped him deal with first-degree murder, it could do wonders for his alibi.

Alibi was a misnomer, though. If the worst happened and the law picked up his trail, his alibi was simply that he couldn't have done it because someone else had: Monica Westfield. He would frame her. She was expendable.

He hoped it didn't come to that. His desire was for life to return to the way it was before the discovery of the bond, before Paul Fontana made his unwelcome intrusion into their lives. Monica had shown interest in stabilizing their relationship even after all they had been through. Marriage sounded acceptable. He still wanted her desperately.

He might become a suspect in Paul's murder, though. This was something he knew from the start, something included in his scheming, a calculated risk. It required a contingency plan, a way to divert attention from himself. A scapegoat. Monica was the logical choice. He had to do it. It was prudent, regardless of its propriety. Another tough choice.

It did no good to relieve himself of deadly ties to Paul Fontana, only to create a new bond with the long arm of the law, one that would have him running and scheming again. He refused to spend his life in jail. What a terrible waste that would be for science, society, and his own life.

In advance, he knew his getaway from the pier and Atlantic City was clean. Right up to nine p.m. that evening, assuming he did nothing radically different to alter the future he'd seen, he was a free man. There was no way to make a connection between Mason and Atlantic City. He knew no one there, and vice versa. There was little evidence to link the two men there together. Paul, though, was known there, a frequent visitor, a habitual gambler. Hopefully, the bit with the poker chips in the mouth, combined with the execution-style, close-range wound to the head, would send authorities off in the wrong direction chasing phantom mob theories. Another poor sap in debt to the wrong crowd, and a message delivered. Mason removed the wallet simply to buy time. With no driver's license or credit cards, identification would be delayed at least a day. He had dropped both the wallet and note in a dumpster at the edge of the parking lot near the car.

Despite his scheming, there was a weak link in his crime, and he knew it. Roger Wilkins. The detective had everything needed to build a compelling case against Mason. The connection between victim and suspect, the opportunity, the weapon, the motive. If the investigator caught wind of the crime through the media, it was unrealistic to count on him forgetting having worked the Brooks case. If he had any scruples, he'd call the police.

Mason pondered ways of preventing this, but concluded it was beyond the range of his ability. It was impossible to shield the man from all media exposure. There were too many ways for him to hear about the crime, and virtually no way short of murder to prevent him from acting on his knowledge.

The answer was to reroute the trail to another suspect, the scapegoat Monica Westfield. He'd taken steps to assure that the authorities followed the leads to her.

He smiled at the thought of Paul's confusion over the strange detour he'd made to the out-of-the-way gas station on the trip to Atlantic City. The purpose had been to drop the credit card he stole out of Monica's purse that morning. Monica wasn't going anywhere and wouldn't notice it missing. There was an excellent chance that some thoughtful motorist or station employee would find the card on the pavement by the gas pumps and report it. Even if they made no effort with it initially, they might make the connection if the media broadcast her name. Perhaps then they would contact the police. Never mind that she made no purchase there with the card, it could have fallen from her purse as she dug for cash. The fact that no one there ever saw her, since she hadn't ever been there, was irrelevant. Not every customer is remembered. There was, though, the chance that once she was connected to a high-profile murder investigation, the memories of attention-seeking employees might miraculously recall her visit. In any event, if found, the card placed her near Atlantic City in the time frame necessary to commit the crime. The odd choice of a station well off the beaten path could be interpreted as an attempt to hide her tracks. It was a clever piece of work.

There was more.

That morning, before admonishing her to stay off the phones, he'd secretly switched off their ringers. She never heard the five calls he made to the house from the casino. The connections were never made, but the telephone company had records of his attempts. If they didn't, he did. Two months earlier, as his paranoia over the bond's threat grew, he had Caller I.D. installed. It recorded those five calls, along with any miscellaneous incoming sales calls, surveys, or charitable donation requests. If the police asked questions, he'd tell them of his repeated attempts to contact her from the casino, how he tried to notify her of Paul's 'disappearance' before giving up and making the return trip alone. He could also provide details on other calls to the house that day. The police could contact those callers and confirm their attempts on the date in question.

If she wasn't answering the phone, where was she?

He was particularly proud of the receipt lying inconspicuously in a basket of bills in a kitchen drawer. He had visited a quickie oil change place with the Mercedes the day before, while Paul and Monica studied at the library. The receipt he got for the work done included the date, the vehicle's license plate number, and most important, its mileage. Afterward, he repeatedly circled the city on the freeway loop, posting enough additional odometer mileage to make a round trip to Atlantic City look possible. If her alibi was that she stayed home the day of the murder, not answering a phone that clearly should have been ringing, while Mason was off driving her car, how could she explain the hundreds of new miles appearing on his car? She couldn't, of course.

It would be difficult for her, too, to explain away her fingerprints on the Mercedes, a car she would no doubt describe as one she never drove. Mason asked her to fetch his driving gloves stuffed above the driver's side visor the night before their trip. If it helped matters, he would deny this event took place. It would be his word against hers, and who was looking like a liar?

A date-stamped parking stub from the casino lot could be found in the Mercedes, stuffed down in the driver's seat. He carried the stub now in his pants pocket and would deposit it in the Mercedes later.

Another subtle touch was the bookstore receipt buried, unbeknownst to Monica, deep in her purse. This could be traced to the purchase of a large, hardcover encyclopedia of handguns, the same book lying in the open in the den, the one Mason bought and read and planted there, hoping Monica would find it and, thinking it strange, pick it up and unwittingly leave a set of fingerprints on the colorful, vinyl sleeve.

That's an odd choice of reading matter, indeed, Ms. Westfield.

As for fingerprints, the most damning evidence was her prints on the murder weapon itself. Monica described to Mason days earlier how she'd handled the gun upon finding it in Paul's room. Those prints were still there.

Mason's prints wouldn't be found on any key evidence. He thoroughly wiped the book sleeve after reading the information he sought and setting it in the study as bait for Monica. He wore the driving gloves during all contact with everything else, receipts, parking stub, credit card, and gun. He was especially careful not to smudge any existing prints on the gun.

Denying he traveled to Atlantic City with Paul would be foolish. With enough sleuthing, he'd probably appear on some surveillance camera in the casino. The story was that he and Paul drove down innocently enough for a day of gambling. Later, Paul disappeared and Mason never saw him again. Monica obviously made the trip down, lured him under the Boardwalk using the note to avoid being seen by Mason, and did him in.

He expected a police investigation competent enough to trace the corpse back to Bally's and discover the baited note scheme. He lacked confidence in their ability to locate the stray patron who delivered the note. With no note to dissect and no witness to Mason's involvement, the police had nothing to go on but the employee's testimony that 'some woman had a note delivered and the man left immediately after reading it, as if to meet her.'

There was slight risk that Paul would discard the note at the casino, leaving it for later discovery. Or that the employee might raise suspicion about the note having been typewritten and lacking signature. Or more remote, that the police might locate the crumpled note in the parking lot dumpster. Assuming the police lab linked the note to the Brooks household, they would find no fingerprints and conclude that Monica had the same availability to the paper and typewriter as he. Suspicion would still be on Monica.

He could provide motive too. There were several to pick from. The obvious was that she'd acted to protect Mason, fervently believing the dream research's prediction that Paul threatened his life, or Paul himself had revealed murderous intent. Another possibility was that she discovered Paul's plan to extort money from Mason, a man she planned to wed, money she felt would soon be lawfully hers. Perhaps their short-lived affair had not gone as hoped. Maybe he jilted her, and she lashed out with the force of a woman scorned. What if the event at Paul's apartment that night had been against her will, and she avenged her rape? There could be others.

When the police investigation got to the right point, Mason would drop one of these gems into the mix. He could choose the optimal one based on the circumstances at the time, or he could dump them all in and let the police try to sort the confusion. All evidence against her was circumstantial, his word against hers, but he'd set her up well. With his ability to control events day-to-day, he could build reasonable doubt on his own guilt, and probably flat out convict her. His reviews allowed him to see troublesome developments in the investigation in advance. He could act to prevent them. A missed meeting here, a dropped hint there. He'd always have plenty of time to thoroughly think through every question asked of him.

She didn't stand a chance.

He hoped it didn't come to that, but there were worse things. With the bond gone, he was now free to pursue any number of enticing things, including other beautiful young women. The world was his.

He thought it odd that Paul chose not to bring his gun to Atlantic City. It didn't matter. Mason didn't need to understand the man's reasoning. He dreamed that when he went to get the gun, it was there, and the fact that he carried it to the casino rather than Paul raised no suspicions. Obviously Paul hadn't checked on it before leaving it behind. The plan could have worked even if Paul took the gun, although it would have left his position weaker. It would have required that Mason obtain another weapon. Monica's fingerprints wouldn't be on the murder weapon. As it was, using Paul's gun for the shooting fit perfectly. Back home he would plant the gun in the drawer as if it never moved. Even Monica would have trouble suspecting him.

Monica might become suspicious when he returned without Paul, but not necessarily. She didn't know that he knew about her affair with Paul. She probably knew nothing about the extortion. In her mind, the bond could be the only motive for Mason to commit such a crime. But why would he do it when success appeared so close? Was there anything in his background or personality that made such behavior possible? He was an elderly, English gentleman, a scientist, not a violent, cold-blooded murderer.

After replacing the gun in Paul's room, he would ask her to check on it as an afterthought to Paul's disappearance. The fact that the weapon would be right where she last saw it would serve to lessen any suspicion of him. If he had killed Paul, what had he done it with? Her peek into the dark cavity behind the drawer would also be an opportunity to refresh her fingerprints on the gun.

Even if Monica did suspect Mason, what would she do about it? She stood to lose much if their happy household disintegrated, as it would if Mason was convicted of murder. She'd proposed marriage just the day before. She understood the threat Paul represented to Mason's life. She had nowhere to go, and had no one to answer to for less-than-scrupulous behavior like overlooking a justifiable homicide here or there if it improved her situation. He could easily see her holding suspicions to herself or being openly supportive, rather than seeking to bring justice.

The reality was, whether Wilkins or Monica went to the law, all circumstantial evidence still pointed to her. It would be trickier to convince anyone of her guilt if she went to the police, but it could be interpreted as an amateurish attempt on her part to frame Mason for a crime she had committed, a classic hey-how-could-I-have-done-it-if-I-came-to-you defense.

Mason was ready and able to handle Monica either way. He would stay near her over the next few days, watching closely, dreaming, and manipulating the future as needed to assure his continued freedom.

Matters would go better for Monica Westfield if no one came to suspect Mason.

Chapter 25

Deep in thought, Monica had lost touch with time and the day slipped past her. She spent the hours alternating between pacing and sitting. The sound of the front door opening snapped her out of the stupor. Glancing at her watch, she was surprised to find that it was quarter to nine. The rumbling in her stomach now reminded her of the dinner she had yet to eat.

She stood and walked quickly to the foyer.

Mason was there, closing the door and switching on the outside lights for the night. The unexpected sight of him was like cold water in the face. Without thinking, she rushed to him and hugged him vigorously.

"Oh Mason, I was so worried about you."

"Why is that?" he said, calmly squeezing her in return.

"I don't know. I started worrying about Paul and the bond. It's so close to nine. I wondered if you'd make it back in time. Foolish, I suppose, but I thought maybe something would happen to you. You shouldn't have gone."

"You might be right," he said, pushing past her into the hall-way.

"What do you mean?" She stood looking at the door. It then occurred to her that he'd locked it. "Where's Paul?"

"Exactly." He said it over his shoulder out of the side of his mouth, with a tone of exasperation.

Monica spun around and strode up to Mason quickly, taking his arm and turning him to face her.

"Where is Paul, Mason?" She said it urgently.

They stood toe-to-toe, staring into each other's eyes.

"I wish I knew where he is, Monica. He was losing badly all day. I left him for a higher-stakes table. Sometime in the middle of the afternoon I lost track of him. He just disappeared. I searched the whole casino for him a dozen times and checked out at the car another half-dozen. The bloody fool took off on me."

Paul's disappearance was like a jolt from an electric fence to Monica. She opened her mouth three times before saying anything.

"You left him there?"

"What else could I do, dear? I had to get back for my recording. He knew that. We set up a meeting time and place. He didn't come. Besides, the casino isn't that big. If he were there, I would have found him. He's a big boy and he knows his way around Atlantic City. He can take care of himself."

"Did you have him paged?"

Mason looked away. "I'm telling you, he wasn't there, okay?"

Monica studied him hard. "Something's happened to him," she said, thinking out loud.

"I certainly hope so," he said, slapping his gloves on the side of his thigh and stomping a leg. "That irresponsible moron completely ignored my instructions. He could have placed me and the entire research project in jeopardy. I should sack the imbecile."

"It doesn't make any sense. He has nothing to gain by skipping out."

"I don't think Paul Fontana gives much prior thought to his actions. My guess is that he caught scent of one of the many opportunistic young ladies roaming the casinos and began thinking with his phallic lobe, rather than his frontal lobe. He's probably in a motel as we speak, exercising his single talent."

Instantly, Monica's feelings were hurt and her face turned sour. Mason watched her expression and looked utterly surprised by her reaction.

"Why should that bother you, dearie?"

He delivered the question with a condescending tone. There was more there than words. It was an invisible knife poking at the tender flesh of her hidden secrets, probing, testing, threatening.

He knew.

She didn't need to dream in non-REM to see it. He either suspected an affair between her and Paul, or he knew facts. The electric fence became a cattle prod. She must be more careful with her comments and facial expressions.

"I don't think that's necessary. I was thinking of how this affects you, Mason."

He let out a skeptical chuckle and headed for the staircase. "I've got to get into bed. If he shows up, I suppose you'll have to let him in and plug him in upstairs as usual. I need his data, and half a night is better than no night at all."

"I will," she said, picturing a drunken, disheveled, lipstick-smeared Paul Fontana pounding at their locked front door in the wee hours of the morning. How could she have felt anything for the man?

Two steps up the staircase, Mason stopped and threw a question at her. "Where were you today, anyway? I thought I made my instructions this morning abundantly clear. I wanted you by the phone in case I called."

"That's right where I was."

"Is that so? Then why did you not answer the phone all day? I called here repeatedly. I thought maybe there was some chance you'd heard from Paul."

"Mason, I was here all day long, and that phone never rang once."

He scoffed and climbed the remaining stairs, disappearing for the night, although it seemed to her that he took longer to settle in than usual. Footsteps and creaking floorboards went up and down the upstairs hallway, and doors opened and closed. She didn't give the matter much thought at the time. She was too busy trying to keep her head above the avalanche of new information just dumped on her.

Slowly, she returned to the study and took her spot on the sofa where the cushion was already compressed from many hours of her weight. Her head was pounding with a migraine headache, and she planned to grab aspirin for it when she got up next. This was a real-life nightmare, the kind that sets danger in plain view and then puts lead weights in your shoes so you can't possibly outrun it. What was the significance of this new, unexpected development?

Something was wrong. Something didn't fit. Her worst fears—that Paul planned to murder Mason—hadn't come true, and there was solace in that, but a new fear lurked in the shadows of her mind, undefined. She sensed it there, intuition perhaps, but couldn't get her hands around it. In her tortured, tired state she realized she now had to struggle through this issue before any new, comprehensive plan of action could be formed.

Think, Westfield. What is it? What doesn't fit?

She reviewed the known facts, a swirling soup of jigsaw puzzle pieces that would surely illustrate what had happened and what new direction to take if only she could work them into place. For an hour she sat trance-like in the quiet house, mulling things over in her mind.

Then a notion occurred to her like an apparition appearing from the mist. There was something wrong, and she suddenly knew what it was. Mason's behavior and conversation with her upon his return were wrong. Wrong in the sense that they were normal. It hadn't occurred to her right away, and to the average person never would. Conversation with Mason had long since ceased to be normal, and this evening its normality seemed conspicuous and alien.

Mason Brooks continued to develop his precognitive abilities daily. There were few surprises for him anymore. Conversation with him had evolved into discussion of things she was going to say to him. She didn't need to actually say it because he'd already dreamed it. That part of the conversation was unnecessary. They immediately moved to the next stage of discussion. Mason would relay thoughts, feelings, or instructions. Even those he had often thought through earlier.

Tonight, though, there was surprise on his face and his words formed questions. That was what was wrong. Mason didn't need to ask questions because he'd already heard the answers. He shouldn't show surprise. Tonight Monica had viewed facial expressions long absent on Mason. Then it was clear to her what that meant.

He had staged the conversation.

Mason had more than one weakness after all. His ability to lie, at least to Monica, was greatly handicapped by how he could act. Surprise could never be part of the repertoire.

Again she thought through the facts. The two men went off together. Only one returned. Mason called, but the phone never rang. Mason lost track of Paul in the afternoon. Now there was no sign of or word from Paul, a man who still had a large interest in Mason Brooks' business, a man who would not have run off without first coming to take her along. Now Mason was lying about something. She had already considered why Mason had not forseen Paul's disappearance in his review, knowing that his forsight was never perfect. There was something else.

Still it didn't come to her. What did it mean? Why would he lie? He would lie because he knew more about what had happened than he wanted to admit. Why keep knowledge secret? Because it contained incriminating information. What could possibly be incriminating for Mason in this situation?

Then the missing piece of the puzzle fell from the sky like Newton's apple.

The gun had been taken too.

Two men go. One returns. One lies. The bond that ties the two is of death, not friendship. Throw in money, a woman, and one gun. What do you get?

The idea was preposterous. The thought that Mason could be capable of such a thing was inconceivable. Yes, he was a liar and a cad, but what was she thinking here...murder? Could he do it? The motive was undeniably there. The bond! Possibly another, too. Jealousy.

A chill filled her and she began to shake. She remembered the extra activity upstairs after Mason retired for the evening. What had he been doing?

If he killed Paul and lied about it to Monica, it meant he didn't want her to know, couldn't trust her with the secret. If that were true, he would need to replace the gun in the spot she knew it to be in.

She had to know. She rose and headed for the stairs. On her way, she took a short detour, stopping at the phone on the mahogany table beneath a Renoir print of a flower arrangement still-life. On a small, lower shelf the Caller I.D. unit sat hidden from view. She scanned through the eight calls listed for that date. There were five from the Bally's Park Place Casino in Atlantic City and three from names and numbers she didn't recognize. That wasn't possible, she thought. She'd been there all day. She lifted the phone and peered underneath. The ringer was switched off. A shiver ran up her spine. Without flipping the switch back, she set the phone down and headed for the stairs.

At the base of the stairs another revelation stopped her feet, and nearly her heart. Caller I.D. She had forgotten all about it until a moment ago. Of course Mason knew about her and Paul. She'd called him from Paul's apartment, and that confounded device betrayed her. Mason knew she was there, knew she lied, knew everything even as she stood and proposed marriage. That's why he'd voided the will and scheduled the trip to Atlantic City, to eradicate Paul Fontana. Would she be next?

Suddenly the fear that she'd struggled with all day in vain, that Paul would kill Mason, seemed silly in retrospect. Mason was never in any danger, not with his powers. He wouldn't have allowed that, regardless of what Paul's intentions might have been.

Monica climbed the stairs as quietly as possible, worried that

Mason might hear and intercept her. For the second time that day she crept slowly and apprehensively to Paul's room.

She turned the doorknob slowly and gently opened the door, allowing the creaks to blend softly into the nightly noises of an old house on a windy night. She skated across the floor in stocking feet and switched on a lamp atop a stack of electronic equipment between the bed and dresser, hoping to keep light in the hallway to a minimum. Removing the drawer and carefully resting it again on the bureau, she reached in for the gun.

It was there.

There was only one way for that gun to have gotten back to its spot. Mason. The cattle prod became a stun gun.

Just before setting the gun back in the drawer, she smelled a distinctive odor. She brought the revolver to her nose and sniffed. Burnt gunpowder. She stepped over and held the gun under the lamp. Looking closely, she turned it over and studied it. Half cocking the hammer and spinning the cylinder, she saw that there was still a casing in each of the six chambers. Viewing it from the front of the barrel, though, she saw that one chamber was empty. A bullet was missing.

The gun had been fired.

Chapter 26

Paul awoke slowly, each rung in the ladder of awareness greased with fear and nausea.

Then came pain, not localized, but substantial. It was beyond tolerance, and he vomited again and again.

Then he was cold.

Finally he got an eye open.

Sand.

What the hell?

As his vision improved, he checked his surroundings. It was dawn, on a beach. There was the ocean. He was beneath a pier.

Where the heck...?

Then he saw the poker chips in the pool of vomit next to his face. He'd heard of blowing chunks, but this? Had he eaten them? Was that why he was sick? Poker chips will do it every time, he was sure.

Suddenly, the chips were a beacon in the fog. Atlantic City, that's where he was. But eating chips? He must have been winning big, showing off to some woman, maybe drinking too much. He sure felt hung over, but how did he get out here?

There was more, though. The pain. What was that about?

Oh, no. Someone caught up with him. Someone thumped him for an old debt. How bad was it?

At the thought, the pain miraculously concentrated to the upper righthand side of his head. His hand went to it and felt matted, crusty hair. His fingers brought down coagulated blood. Panic, and more nausea.

It came back then, all of it. Mason had shot him. A head wound. God. He imagined part of his skull blown away, a huge gaping wound, important parts exposed, permanent brain damage. Was he paralyzed? He struggled to move his legs. At first they resisted, but eventually he regained feeling and motion...just cold and stiff. Was there a bullet lodged up there? Dare he move?

Again he raised his hand to the wound. Gingerly, he felt around the area. The skull was intact. He probed farther, trying to locate the entry point, but could find no hole. The wound was too tender and his fingers too cold. Strangely, the left side of his head hurt nearly as bad as the right, and when he touched the area he discovered a huge lump, although there was no evidence of bleeding. That remained a mystery only until he noticed the pillar two feet from his head and recalled the vision he'd had immediately before Mason shot him. He'd seen himself charging, Mason firing, and his head striking the post hard.

Could he have been so lucky as to receive only a glancing blow, a skull bouncer? Was he shot in the head at close range only to survive with but a severe concussion?

Must be the hair.

Even as Paul counted his blessings, the enormous significance of the shooting began to sink in. Mason Brooks was deranged, a brilliant madman run amok, a gun-toting evil magician with tendencies toward jealousy and paranoia. The world was in trouble.

Paul looked about in the growing light, expecting to see Mason creeping up on him, intent on finishing the deed. He needed to get up and moving. If Mason didn't come back to kill him, blood-loss or hypothermia would. He felt oddly embarrassed too. Vomiting in the sand wasn't the Paul Fontana way, and he didn't want to be found here in this condition, by anyone. Though still early, someone could come along at any time.

Dizzy, cold, and miserable, Paul reached his feet, giving his first thoughts to his next move. He patted himself down, wiping off the sand and confirming that no other wounds existed. He had apparently not moved after falling in the sand, and lying horizontally, no blood had spilled on his clothes. He was surprisingly neat.

Stiffly, he moved toward the stairs. Six steps later, he toppled in the sand, felled by vertigo.

As he lay there, fighting nausea, he became aware of the blood that had flowed down from the wound and dried to a tight crust all along the side of his face. So much for neat.

He had to get cleaned up before going anywhere. If he got onto the pier looking like this, someone would spot him and call the cops for sure.

What would be wrong with that? His instinct had been to avoid the law, a natural reaction to a lifetime of speeding tickets and efforts to avoid them. This was different, though. He was the victim now. Logically, he should crawl up to the Boardwalk and scream for help and then sic the police on Brooks, make him pay for what he did.

But there had been nothing logical in his life since that first meeting with Brooks only days earlier, a period that now seemed like a lifetime. The police couldn't stop Mason, Paul was sure, not with Mason's power. Mason would know they were coming long before they arrived. He could avoid the police just as effectively as he avoided his own death. Worse yet, he could tell them a tale and turn the tables so completely that they might end up jailing Paul as some raving lunatic. After all, the truth was quite unbelievable.

Reaching his feet again, Paul was filled with anger. His concern for what an unleashed Mason Brooks meant to society suddenly paled in comparison to the anger he felt over what Mason had done to him personally. Brooks tried to murder him. Nobody does that to Paul Fontana. Cops or no cops, Brooks was going to pay.

His next move became clear. Get Brooks.

Surely, Mason would have returned home by now. His equipment was there and, like a vampire returning to the coffin, he must plug himself in for another night's recording to maintain his power and immortality. Getting there was the problem for Paul. Mason had the car. Paul had nothing. He'd need money to accomplish anything now.

He reached for his wallet, only to find it missing, just then recalling its absence during his earlier pat-down. He looked around him in the sand, but knew it wasn't there. He hadn't moved all night. It hadn't fallen out. Brooks took it.

No wallet meant no credit cards or drivers license, which ruled out a rental car. He'd have to take a bus. That required cash. He again felt his empty pockets. His winnings were gone. That slimeball Brooks was a thief too.

His anger turned to rage.

Without hesitation, Paul then did something a thousand dollars and a hundred years would never get him to do. Retracing his steps to the spot where he'd lain in the night, he stooped and sank both hands into his own pool of cold vomit. Retrieving the six, fifty-dollar poker chips, he carried them to the water's edge, where he rinsed and pocketed them, and then did his best to clean the dried blood from his face and hair.

More carefully this time, Paul staggered to the stairs and managed to climb slowly to the pier deck. Once on top, he collapsed onto a bench, exhausted and dizzy. Trying to be inconspicuous, he buried his face in his hands and worked his way through a bout of dry heaves.

This wasn't going to be an easy or pleasant trip.

Using each bench and railing as a goal, Paul picked his way back up the Boardwalk, chopping the journey into many smaller treks with heave and rest breaks between. He needed to make it to the warmth of the casino, where he could wash up more properly in the restroom to avoid attracting unwanted attention. Next, he'd cash in the poker chips and use the money for bus fare home. The sun was up by the time he sat for another rest just outside Bally's Park Place.

As the fog in his mind continued to lift and the previous night's events replayed, Paul recalled the sly smile on Mason's face just before he'd pulled the trigger. There was more to Mason's motivation than jealousy or self-preservation. He had enjoyed it.

That scary revelation led to another. Monica was in danger.

He'd overlooked that aspect in his confusion, and now felt foolish and guilty for thinking only of himself. If Mason was capable of killing Paul, could he not also kill Monica? Ostensibly, he'd shot Paul to break the bond, but what weight in his decision did jealousy hold? Did the same fate await Monica? Was it already too late? He recalled now, in a flood of panicked thoughts, that Mason had gone back into the house briefly before they left for Atlantic City the previous morning. Had he coolly executed her for her role then?

At that moment and for the first time, Paul Fontana felt love for another, true love, love for someone other than himself or his mother. It gripped him by the throat and shook him. Every inch of the great wall around him shattered like glass and fell away, leaving him exposed and vulnerable. He felt fear greater than fear of personal injury, greater than his fear over the death of his mother—that fear that had dogged him forever and suddenly no longer mattered. He feared for another, the one he loved unconditionally. Monica Westfield.

Instantly, the pain subsided and he was oblivious to the cold. All thoughts and concerns fell secondary to the urgent need to rescue her. With great conscious effort he tried to harness his rage, to apply it with reason, to prevent its throwing him headlong into some fruitless act that might jeopardize both their lives.

He hoped with every fiber that she still lived, but even if she were alive and Mason had no intention of killing her now, she was still in mortal danger. She would surely suspect Mason of something when he returned without Paul, and would definitely know the truth when Paul showed up alive to tell it. Mason would have to deal with her somehow. She didn't love Mason, that was clear, and couldn't continue the charade for long. How would

Mason react to and deal with her rejection of him? Paul knew the answer. Like Mason had said to Paul, it was only a matter of time. Paul had to get her out.

Please, don't let it be too late.

There may be time. He guessed that Mason, after the shooting the night before, had arrived at his lab just in time to hook himself up for non-REM recording and probably wouldn't have taken further drastic action that late in the day so close to his 'grey zone' of nine p.m. He would rely on another night's monitoring to guide his actions the following day. That day was today. There was no time to waste.

Entering the casino and passing a pay phone, Paul considered and rejected the idea of calling the Brooks home to check on Monica's welfare and warn her. His only hope was the element of surprise, and that only existed as long as Mason still believed, as he obviously did, that Paul was dead. He couldn't risk the consequences of Mason answering the phone and somehow identifying the caller as Paul, or Monica somehow tipping Mason through words, expressions or action as a result of speaking to Paul.

Paul had to deal with this face to face. What he could do, injured, unarmed, and without benefit of a review, against the power and foresight of Mason Brooks—not to mention the .38 caliber Smith & Wesson—was unknown. It didn't matter. He had to try.

One way or another, Paul was determined to make it back, and Mason would have to shoot him dead to stop him from saving Monica.

This time he better not miss.

If having no car or money had seemed like difficult problems to overcome, they were nothing compared to Paul's next sudden realization.

Mason would see Paul coming.

That power would work against Paul the same as it did against the police or Mason's own death. In fact, if Paul confronted Mason later in the day, Mason could this very moment be learning about it and planning Paul's defeat.

The thought was overwhelming. How do you beat this guy? He needed an angle, an edge, a plan. There must be a way. Don't give up. Think.

Unfortunately, vertigo was the result of his deepest thinking, and it struck again as he leaned through a restroom door. Passing the mirror on his way to a stall, he was shocked at his true appearance. Neat, indeed. He looked dead. It was lucky that he'd gotten as far as he did without attracting attention. Only the quiet of the early hour had saved him. The place was virtually empty.

The absolute need to avoid the interest of police or other concerned citizens really sank in then. No one could help him save Monica. All they could do was delay his own attempt and possibly tip Mason to Paul's survival.

He took a short rest in the stall, soaking-in the room's warmth and feeling color return to his skin. Then he approached the sink and did a better job of cleaning up than on the beach.

After closely inspecting the wounds on the sides of his head and concluding they would not be fatal, Paul stood staring at himself in the mirror. There had been many hours spent in front of mirrors before, but this was different. This time there was no primping the hair, no flexing of muscles, no sucking in the belly, or fretting over wrinkles. He was mesmerized by the eyes and what was hidden behind them.

You almost died last night, Fontana. Maybe part of you did die out there. It would be hard not to be changed by something like that. Now it was time to grow up, time to get serious.

For the moment, serious meant finding a way past Mason's defenses.

The eyes. He kept staring into his own eyes. There's something in there. You know something, Fontana, don't you? How could you know something? How is it possible to know something, yet not know what it is?

He remembered what Mason had said about the research, that the entire process of non-REM recall was learned. Over time the mind became trained to transfer non-REM images to the conscious present, and required less stimulus to do so.

Could he be feeling a leaking non-REM dream? Was he sensing something significant about the day's future, a weak 'general feel for the day,' despite not having had a review? How could that be possible when Mason had been at this for over a year and still hooked up every night and every morning? Paul had only done the process a few times.

Just maybe it could work. Most of Mason's earlier reviews were ineffective as he tweaked the process. He wasn't surprised by Paul's rapid success because Paul received state-of-the-art treatments, and he clearly feared that Paul would soon possess equal powers. Paul was a good student, a quick study. Perhaps Mason, too, might see the future without a formal review if only he tried. His dependence on the equipment held him back. He probably had considered this and planned to experiment accordingly, but only after breaking the bond. Facing the threat of death, he wouldn't risk one night away from his trusty equipment.

That's great, Fontana. You're thinking big now, but what does it all mean? The future will be revealed to you later? That's not good enough. What do you feel now?

He stared so hard he was squinting.

Go! That's what he saw. He'd have to go after her. That's all he felt. He'd have to trust it. Maybe there would be a deja vu flash or two to clarify things later. For now he'd just have to do it. If he were truly sensing the future at some level and there was impending doom ahead, that's what he should feel now, but he didn't.

Mason had said to trust instincts.

So we go in. Good plan, John Wayne.

In truth, he realized, all his clever thoughts were immaterial. What else could he do? Go get her, or run away. Those were the choices.

Paul Fontana was no rabbit.

He used the hand drier to warm and dry his hands, and then

proceeded to the nearest cashier's window out the door and to his right. He was apprehensive about his appearance and how the woman in the booth would react to the sight of him. Knowing he didn't look good, he hoped she'd simply take him for another all-nighter who'd had too much to drink before cashing in his last half-dozen chips.

He began to feel poorly again as he neared the cashier. He'd spent too much time standing in the restroom. Things began to spin again. He held the six chips in his hand, ready to plop them down, hoping to speed the process.

Ten feet from her, he made eye contact with the unoccupied cashier. Stressed by the impending transaction and the conse-quences of his wound being obvious, he felt a little shot of adren-aline. It didn't help his condition.

Five feet and the room began to go dim at the edge of his vision. He felt feverish and weak. He considered returning to the restroom for a break before trying again, but could see her look-ing at him oddly. He was committed.

Two feet and the cashier stood and was saying something to him, but he heard no words. He tried to raise his hand and place the chips on the counter, but strangely, the chips were now scat-tered on the tile floor, rolling and wobbling.

How did they get there?

Then everything went black.

Chapter 27

Mason sat at his roll-top desk with a hand on one of the three phones in the house. He'd switched the ringers of two phones back on the night before, and reminded himself to take care of the third, downstairs, later.

None of that really mattered anymore, though. There was a change of plans.

The night before was as bizarre as any Mason had ever experienced. Wildly exciting REM dreams filled the night, playing out exotic sexual fantasies resulting in his first wet dream in forty-five years. The messy nocturnal emission amused rather than embarrassed him, as it might have under other circumstances. Nothing seemed to embarrass him anymore. If it had, his erotic dreams wouldn't have reached their climactic proportions.

There was another unusual aspect of the REM dreams. Violence. Some contained only minor aggression, dominance over the women participants, verbal abuse, rough handling. This type of dream had occurred more frequently in recent months, but never so vividly, and never leaving him with such a feeling of power and satisfaction. Most interesting were his dreams of felonious violence: assault, rape, murder. He was the offender, unstoppable, remorseless. He expected his REM dreams that night to synthesize the dirty business of Paul Fontana in Atlantic City into something rational, to imprint a memory record a sane mind and healthy superego could cope with, but there was no sign of it. The only connection, perhaps, was the other violent dreams.

The REM dreams were vivid and potent, causing high conscious retention of specific scenes and leaving a residual excitement in his waking hours. He carried that mood into his non-REM review, and it was still with him now, heightened by the revelations offered by his non-REM replay.

His non-REM dreams, too, had been unusual. They started with power and clarity, defining exactly what he would do that morning. At some point later in the review, however, there was a significant change, one he hadn't previously experienced and didn't understand. He saw himself back at home, having completed important tasks yet ahead of him that morning, when suddenly an overwhelming sense of serenity engulfed him. A calm, like floating, disembodied, in a cloud. Everything was shadowed and he couldn't quite see what was ahead. There was an odd quality to it, as if something pleasant and special were to happen. He assumed it was the sense of completion and security he'd surely feel after achieving his goals for the day. He planned to study his EEG printouts later, something he'd been lax at since relying so heavily on his reviews and investing the time to study Paul's results so meticulously. Maybe he would find something of interest there, something to shed light on the mysterious unknown ahead. There was no time to check the printouts now, though. And, certainly, he felt no cause for concern. His review had not revealed trouble ahead for him, only for others.

He rummaged through a bin at the back of the roll-top and found what he was looking for, a business card from Roger Wilkins, private detective. Picking up the receiver, he dialed the second number listed, Wilkins' home number. Wilkins answered after four rings.

"Roger, this is Mason Brooks," he said with urgency. "I need to meet with you right away."

Wilkins hesitated. "Um...It's Sunday morning, Mister Brooks. I can't see you now. I don't work on Sundays."

"But this is an emergency. Something has come up, and it's very important that I see you now."

"Mason, I have commitments with my family. I'm sure you understand. It can wait until tomorrow, can't it?"

"No, it cannot. It's imperative that I meet with you immediately...and privately. No one must know."

"What's this about?"

"I can't talk about it now, and won't talk about it over the phone."

Wilkins sighed at the other end of the line and said nothing. Mason persisted.

"Come, man, I'll triple your daily rate. Give me one hour of your time."

Another hesitation, and then, "Brooks, I'm serious, I'm going to bill you the whole thing, three days, if you insist on this. I'm not in the business of—"

"How soon can you be at your office?"

"Forty-five minutes."

"Make it thirty."

He hung up the phone and smiled a crooked smile.

Perfect.

Once downstairs, dressed and ready to go, he poked his head through the swinging door to the kitchen. Monica was there, drinking coffee at the island counter, about to take on the morning newspaper. She looked up with a strange expression on her face.

"Did our playboy friend return to the nest in the night?"

Monica shook her head, her eyes fixed on Mason.

Mason snorted in disgust. "Well, isn't that just fine. There goes the whole research project." He mumbled a few rare expletives for effect. "I need to go out for a while."

Monica set her cup down quickly and appeared concerned. "Where are you going?" she asked.

"I won't be gone more than an hour, I would think. Please stay around the house. I may need you later."

She stood to ask more questions, but Mason stepped back out of the doorway, letting the door swing shut after him. He walked quickly out of the house and climbed into his car.

The drive across town went smoothly. A light snow was falling and enough had accumulated on the roads to make them slick, but the winds were calm and the traffic sparse. Wilkins' office was uptown in a two-level strip-mall, the kind that clung to the sides of each main artery in and out of town like a rash spreading into the suburbs. When he arrived, there was only one other car in the lot, parked up near the front door leading to the office suites on the second level. The flower shop and liquor store on either side were closed, as were all the storefronts. The car's engine was running and Wilkins was at the wheel, trying to stay warm.

The man was punctual. Mason appreciated that. He pulled up alongside the car and parked.

They got out and Wilkins keyed the lock to the front door and led him upstairs to his office, neither man saying a word. This was Mason's third visit to the small suite down the hall to the right. From the hallway the view was far from the stereotypical, dark and dingy private eye office, but inside the clutter and disorganization evoked an image closer to Hollywood's version. They passed through the outer reception area and into Roger's private office, where he rounded the desk and sat with his back to a window overlooking the parking lot below. The desk was a seventies-vintage sheet metal affair with its simulated wood vinyl top peeled up on the corners, revealing chipboard below. It was piled high with stacks of files and paper. A bank of three file cabinets was to his right. Some boxes, more manila file stacks, and a neglected plant rode atop these. Cheesy flea market art hung on the wall, and a pair of garage-sale chairs tried to fill the space of what could have been an attractive office in the right care.

Mason pulled a chair up to the front of the desk and sat heavily.

"Now, Mister Brooks, what's this about?"

Mason took a deep breath and started in. "I think perhaps my wife has committed murder."

Wilkins tried unsuccessfully to appear unfazed by the statement. His eyebrow rose and fell. He blinked a few times and
pursed his lips. He leaned back into the chair and put his arms
behind his head.

"That sounds like a matter for the police. Why don't you go to
them? If I find out it's true, that's what I'll do anyway."

"No, not yet. I don't know for sure, and I must know before the
police are involved. My marriage could hardly benefit from a
false accusation of murder."

"I see your point. Would this be the party you hired me to
investigate for you earlier?"

"That's correct."

"What makes you suspect your wife has murdered Fontana?"

"You may be surprised to know that you were not retained initially because I suspected my wife of infidelity. Rather, Mister
Fontana fit the profile of an ideal subject for a research project I
was conducting on dream analysis. I needed your investigation to
confirm aspects of his personality and lifestyle. I then hired him
and brought him into my home to conduct the research. It was
only then, a matter of days later, that I asked you to watch the two
of them. Despite the unfortunate result you reported to me, I was
forced, for the sake of the project, to overlook their activities and
keep him on in the house. I'm not sure what her motive may be
for what she has done, but there is ample matter there to forge a
few good ones. She may have had a falling out with him, or a late
twinge of guilt over what she'd done, deciding that he was
responsible for her temporary lapse of propriety. It's possible,
too, that whatever occurred in his apartment that evening was
against her will. He may have been envious of me and planning
some evil act that she interceded on. It's difficult to say what
motivated her."

"You say you're not sure she committed the murder. Is that
because you're not sure she did it, or because there's no body
yet?"

"The latter."

"Then why the suspicion?"

"Fontana and I traveled by car to Atlantic City together yesterday to visit a casino. He disappeared and I was forced to return alone. There's been no sign of him since."

"That's not much of a case. I can see why you didn't go to the police."

"No, no. You don't understand. We took her car and left mine here with her. This morning there were hundreds of extra miles on mine, enough for a trip down there and back. Remember the gun? After Paul and I were in the car, set to leave for Atlantic City, I made up an excuse to go back into the house for something I'd forgotten. I checked on his gun in its hiding spot, and it was there. This morning, although he has not returned, it's missing. I didn't take it. She's the only other one who knew of it. Plus, there was a new book on handguns in the study that she must have just purchased and was reading. That is not a subject matter she would normally have an interest in."

"So you think she sneaked down there after you, spirited him away, and shot him with his own gun."

"Yes."

"That's awful thin, Brooks. It might be your imagination just working a little overtime. Our discovery came as a shock to you, no doubt."

"Perhaps."

"Have you confronted her on this?"

"No. I must know the truth first."

"So you've come to me for that."

"Precisely."

"Then I would propose that the first course of action be to locate Mister Fontana. No?"

"Yes."

"Have you checked for him at his apartment?"

"No. I'm afraid I've misplaced his phone number and address. I was hoping you retained a record of your investigation."

"You haven't even called him to see if he went home? I'm sure he's in the book."

"I'm sure he's not there."

"Well, let's find out. We'll call him from right here, and if he answers, this is going to be one expensive phone call for you, Mister Brooks."

Wilkins rose and stepped to his right, unlocking the center file cabinet. Pulling out a lower drawer and bending over, he thumbed through files until he found the one containing the record of his investigation of Paul Fontana.

This was what Mason came for. He rose and circled the desk, standing behind Wilkins. Without hesitation he drew the revolver he had again borrowed from Paul Fontana's room that morning. Reaching downward at arm's length, he stuck the end of the barrel at the base of Roger Wilkins' brainstem and fired one shot.

The combination of anticipating the scene he knew was coming and witnessing it live made the action doubly thrilling for Mason. Roger Wilkins was dead before his one-hundred-ninety-pound frame collapsed onto the open drawer, causing a loud chain-reaction of falling items. His limp deadweight on the lower drawer toppled the file cabinet forward, sending the boxes, stacks of files, and potted plant sprawling across his back and onto the floor. One box landed on the desk, continuing the domino effect on all the files stacked there. It was five seconds before all movement in the room ceased.

Mason's second murder was quite a different affair from the first. The sole shot in the fading light on the shore in Atlantic City had been drowned out by the wind and surf, a pop in the night, a soft body thumping onto the soft beach. The business with Roger Wilkins, however, was shocking and anything but sanitized. In the silent, closed-in office the gun's report had been deafening, leaving his right ear on the gun-hand side ringing painfully. The mess of paper and potting soil on the floor gave the whole scene the appearance of something far more involved than a single shot, as if the room were ransacked and the man beaten.

Mason stood and took it all in. He was in no hurry. No one had heard. There was no one in the building, and no one would come for hours, probably not until morning.

He stooped and picked his file out of the rubble, taking his time and looking closely at the wound in Roger's head. Surprisingly, he didn't find it distasteful, but instead, intriguing, compelling. There was an excitement that went far beyond boyish curiosity. Something was stirring within him, something deep, ancient, instinctive. He didn't want to leave. There was a morbid desire to stay and study the face with its odd expression, eyes half open and mouth ajar.

Mason had what he came for. He had dreamt this event the night before in non-REM, and it made sense. Despite his plotting and scheming, there remained an audit trail of tangible evidence linking him to the murder of Paul Fontana, one he couldn't allow to exist outside his control. Roger Wilkins' file on his investigation of Paul. One thing led to another. The simplest way to get the file was the direct way, right from the source. That, of course, meant terminating Wilkins as well. With Wilkins gone, eliminated, too, was any chance of being connected to Paul's murder. It was logical. His new super-id made it possible. It was simply something he didn't think of before completing the first homicide, couldn't have imagined himself doing. He'd discovered something interesting in Atlantic City, though. Killing someone wasn't nearly as difficult or stressful a task as he had believed.

He took another look at Wilkins and then admitted to himself that his original plot was probably adequate to leave him free of suspicion in Paul's murder. The real reason he was here was something else. He wanted to kill someone.

One last look, and then he left the office, closing and locking both the inner and outer doors as he went. Outside, the snow had picked up. Within an hour or two there would be no trace of his tire tracks in the lot.

Driving home he took a detour to the parking lot of a closed convenience store and buried the file in its dumpster.

He spent the rest of the drive home fleshing out two new thoughts that occurred to him. One was that he had no reason to share his discovery of the true nature of non-REM dreams with the world. At least not now. There would be time for that later. Earlier, as the research began showing promise, he'd imagined the press conference he would hold at the university in which he would enlighten the world with what he'd learned. There would be grants to follow, more book contracts, fame, maybe even a Nobel Prize. None of that mattered anymore. Money was of no concern, and drawing attention to himself was the last thing he wanted. The power his discovery offered was not to be shared. It was its secret existence that made it so valuable, the element of surprise, the ability to do and know things that no one else could imagine or believe possible. As he had learned, more than one person with the ability made controlling the future much more difficult. Why should he subject himself to that? What did he stand to gain? As it now stood, the world was his personal play- ground. He was untouchable, except for one problem. Monica.

That was his second thought. It was clear now. Monica must die. She was the only living person who knew of his abilities. She was the only person who could possibly link him to Paul's mur- der, now two murders. He couldn't trust her. She was the weak link. She was beautiful, he loved her, and he hated to waste all that. But why risk it? Only she could bring him down. The cam- puses of the world were full of young Monicas, impressionable, innocent, beautiful, voluptuous. Suddenly it seemed ridiculous to restrict himself to only one. Besides, killing her would be fun.

Tomorrow he would do the deed. Tonight he would dream it in non-REM and work out the angles so the crime was flawless and he could again be above reproach, walking free into a new life, unhindered by the chains of responsibility, relationships, or remorse. At that moment he felt immortal.

Chapter 28

For the second time that day, Paul climbed the greased ladder to consciousness. This time, though, he heard voices along the way, little snippets of conversation.

"John Doe...probable gunshot...life signs stable."

Also different this time, when fully awake he found himself in a brightly-lit room.

One quick look around and it was clear. He was in a hospital. He must have passed out. There was another bed to his right. The person in it was out cold, asleep, or worse. A nurse was in the room too, sticking items from a rolling cart into a lower cabinet along the wall. She finished and left the room without paying him any attention.

Assessing his personal condition, he found his head bandaged and an I.V. in his left arm. His head was still quite painful, but overall he felt much better.

Drugs, he guessed.

The clock on the wall snapped him to action. Eleven-fifty a.m. He'd been out for hours, crucial hours, that might mean the difference between life and death for Monica.

He drew back the covers to find himself dressed in nothing but a tie-in-the-back hospital gown. His clothes were gone, shoes and all. Tentatively, he sat up and swung his legs down. Woozy but capable, he stood and drew a few deep breaths. He took a step toward the door, forgetting the I.V. still stuck in his arm, and almost pulled the saline bag and stand crashing to the floor. The action wrenched his arm and the sharp pain almost felled him. Carefully, he drew back the tape and withdrew the plastic tube. Blood began to ooze out immediately. He sealed the hole as best he could with the surgical tape, but soon blood was dripping down his arm.

He tiptoed to the door and cracked it open, peeking out in both directions down the hall. Forty feet to his left, a cop was leaning over the counter at a nurse's station. From his casual stance, it appeared he was there for the duration and filling in time flirting with nurses. He might even have been assigned to watch Paul.

To the right, the long hall was empty. At the end and on the opposite side was a door with a red exit sign overhead.

Paul eased the door shut. He had to get to that exit, but he needed cover.

He went to the cabinets along the wall and began searching for anything helpful. He found something almost immediately. A green surgical suit, complete with smock, billowy pants, matching cap, and elastic booties.

Stepping into a side bathroom to change, he saw himself in the mirror for the first time since the casino. His color hadn't improved much. The head bandage consisted of a gauze square attached with surgical tape. His head had been shaved on the right side, presumably to allow cleaning and dressing of the wound.

Oh, no, not the hair.

Even with the green cap, the bandage would attract attention and had to go. Gingerly he peeled off the tape, hoping not to expose the gray noodle. To his surprise there wasn't much to the wound. He didn't think it would show, at least not from a distance. What stood out was the shaved head, which wouldn't have been so bad, maybe even fashionable, if they'd bothered to even out the cut by shaving both sides, but apparently the bump on his left side didn't require repair. There was no way to fix that now, and no time to worry about it.

Wiping the bloody arm on a towel first, he quickly donned the medical suit and returned to the door for another peek. The situation remained unchanged.

After another deep breath, he nonchalantly opened the door and strode into the hall, hoping no one would see him. If they did, he hoped they didn't notice he was naked and barefoot under the green suit. Turning to his right, he made for the exit without so much as a turn of the head. Ten feet from his own room his heart stopped. A door ahead of him opened and the nurse who had just been in his room walked out and turned in his direction, pushing the cart ahead of her.

He allowed his eyes to drop down enough to peek at his left arm. Blood was soaking through the sleeve. Fighting off panic, he raised his eyes and kept walking.

The nurse smiled at him as she passed.

Finally, he reached the end of the hall. He opened the door and, just before going through, ventured a peek back down the hall. The cop was still there. So far so good.

The door opened to a stairwell that spiraled down clockwise. He started down immediately, grasping the inside railing tightly and picking his footing carefully. Looking down, it appeared that he was three or four flights up.

Great. What else could happen?

Unfortunately, he thought of something as soon as the question popped. His free hand dropped to where his pockets should be. There were none.

Sure. His pants were gone, and so were his poker chips. He thought about going back to the room to look for them, but decided against it. It was too risky. Besides, there was a high probability that he'd been whisked away from the casino without regard to the chips strewn on the floor. No chips meant no cash, no bus fare, and no way home.

He shook his sore head. All that cold vomit for nothing.

He'd have to keep moving and figure things out as he went.

Halfway down, a door he'd just passed opened and someone

entered the stairwell and started down after him. The person moved more quickly than Paul could and soon overtook him. With heart racing, Paul lifted his left hand to his face and rubbed his chin in a mock display of pensive, slow-walking contemplation, hoping to hide the bloodstained arm, a surgeon deep in thought between carvings.

The orderly passed on Paul's left with a polite "Hi," obviously missing the damage and odd haircut above Paul's right ear.

The stairwell was empty when Paul reached the last step. Two doors were there to choose from. One was against the outside wall with an exit sign overhead. The other presumably opened to another hallway or part of the hospital. Paul didn't bother to find out which. Going through the exit door, he found himself on a concrete walkway that appeared to lead around toward the front of the building on the left. The walkway was empty and didn't seem well traveled. Paul had chosen his exit well.

To his right was a small patio with two wrought-iron benches, a birdbath, and shrubbery. Its perimeter was lined with a mix of groomed Pagoda Dogwoods and Columnar Buckthorns that created a sense of seclusion. He stepped onto the patio and backed into a corner of the brush, trying to decide his next move.

He'd have to do something fast. It wouldn't be long before he'd be noticed missing. He could see his breath in the cold air. The concrete patio stones felt like block ice through the disposable paper booties. His head throbbed and his arm was a mess, although he clearly wasn't about to bleed to death from it. His costume would attract attention anywhere but at the hospital, and in this temperature and in his condition, he wouldn't get far on foot. He needed wheels. Hitchhiking wasn't an option.

He crossed the patio toward the back of the building and slipped through the bushes. Stopping at the corner, he hid behind another Buckthorn. In the back was a rear parking lot and the hospital's emergency entrance. An ambulance and squad car sat in the turnaround, their engines off. A woman in street clothes had just parked and was scurrying toward the building with a look of concern. She disappeared inside, and then the lot was silent and still.

It was cold. Have to do something, and do it now, Fontana.

On the opposite side of the turnaround and emergency entrance, another ambulance was backed into a parking spot. Without a clear plan, he chose that direction. The vehicle may be open. It offered shelter, a bit of warmth, blankets maybe, a place to lie down. Perhaps it wouldn't be used for a while and he could hide out. No good, he thought. Need to keep moving. There was no time to waste hiding. He had to get to Monica. Maybe the paramedics would go out on a call and he could stow away.

Forget it, just get to the damn ambulance and we'll decide from there. One step at a time.

Paul stepped out from behind his bush onto the sidewalk along the parking lot and casually strode past the emergency entrance. No one seemed to notice him. He came up to the back of the ambulance and peered through the rear window. It was empty. When he tried the door, it opened. Just in case someone was watching him from a window, he pretended to be adjusting things inside, and then climbed in. He waited a moment before pulling the door shut.

It was warmer inside and he was out of view, but this was going nowhere. He needed to be on the Parkway, and soon. He moved to the front of the vehicle to watch any activity outside that might give him an idea. Then he saw them. The keys.

They'd left the keys in the ignition. He pondered this for a moment, and then turned aside and shrugged at an invisible partner. Why not?

Slipping into the driver's seat, he fired the engine and calmly eased out of the parking lot.

This is grand theft auto, Fontana. You understand that's peanuts compared to what'll happen if you don't get north in time, but how do you explain it to the cops?

Turning up and down various streets, trying to orient himself, he thought through what to say if pulled over. He was deranged from the bump on his head? He just wanted to return to the casino to retrieve his chips? This hospital doesn't participate in his HMO? There was nothing he could say. They wouldn't believe the truth. No, getting pulled over meant going downtown, and this time there would be no getting away. Monica couldn't afford that delay.

He wasn't sure which hospital he'd been at, but didn't think it would be far from the strip. Within a few minutes of aimless wandering he found a sign leading him out of town and onto the Parkway.

In a rare piece of good fortune, the gas gauge read full.

After some internal debate over whether it was more prudent to drive with or without the lights flashing, he opted for the lights. He might attract more attention that way, but it was the only way he could drive ninety-five miles an hour and get away with it.

Paul flipped the flashing lights switch on, sounded the siren, and stomped on the gas.

Chapter 29

Monica thought everything through ten times, a hundred times. She had no choice. It came down to courage, not decision. Her plan made sense, but logic and reason were luxuries only others could afford. In the presence of Mason Brooks they were useless frills, lacy adornments to dress in, on the walk down life's path, serving only to delude the unsuspecting into believing they control their own destiny. Only Mason controlled destiny.

That made what she was about to do insane.

Mason had returned at midmorning in a strange mood. He wasn't inclined to tell where he'd been, and she didn't probe. It hardly mattered at this point. She did her best to remain calm and mask her convictions on the evil he had perpetrated. She kept up a light chatter on a variety of topics, all designed to direct conversation away from Paul's whereabouts or anything to do with non-REM research.

She needed to buy time.

She talked about wedding dresses and what she wished for in a ceremony. She asked him what he wanted for Christmas and suggested they string lights along the railing on the front stoop, something they had never done before. She made hot chocolate, which they shared in front of a cozy fire in the study. She knew his powers were as active as ever when she rose to brew it, because he asked her to drop marshmallows in the cups too, though she hadn't explained what she was up to.

Mason was unusually pleasant, smiling and talking with her, even flirting. Standing in the kitchen at one point, he came up behind her and stroked her hair and placed his hands on her shoulders. She managed not to cringe. He spoke an open-ended statement, "Maybe tonight, since Paul is out of the house...."

She forced a smile and answered seductively, "Maybe."

She did what she could to keep him at ease and preoccupied, always watching him closely, listening for a hint of change.

The change she was looking for came dramatically shortly after two in the afternoon. They were discussing politics in the usual fashion, Mason responding to her comments and questions before she made them, when he suddenly sat straight up and said, "Oh," as if he'd been poked in the back. He looked at her blankly for a moment, and then followed it with, "Good god, no."

A panicked look filled his eyes and he stood and ran from the room. Monica followed closely behind.

"What's the matter, dear?"

Mason didn't answer. Instead he charged up the stairs and veered left toward his lab. When Monica caught up to him, he was standing by his bed, studying the EEG readouts he had neglected to review earlier, and swearing profusely.

"What is it, Mason?"

He held a handful of the thin, six-foot-long printout and thrust it in her direction. "It's this! You get to ten after two p.m. and it stops. It's not even flatline after that, it just stops." He dropped it and checked the tape output of several other recording devices. "They're all the same."

"What does it mean?"

"It means, you ignorant cow, that I have no idea what will happen for the rest of the day. Somehow the equipment all failed at precisely the same time of night and only recorded the non-REM activity that shows what takes place through early afternoon today. I didn't check these readouts this morning when I should have. I noticed something different during review, but didn't make much of it. I felt a nothingness, as if there was a long, serene, uneventful period during the day. Now I know why. I felt the change downstairs at ten past two. It was like a light going off. I instantly lost all sense of what was coming."

He swore again and rushed to the other side of the bed, tinkering with wires and switches, checking connections, tapping volume unit meters, desperately trying to determine how equipment that was now perfectly operational could have failed in the middle of the night at such a critical time.

This was Monica's cue. She now knew what she needed to know. Slipping out of the room unnoticed by Mason, she scurried down the hall and into Paul's room. Quickly removing the dresser drawer again, she pulled the revolver from its niche.

As an afterthought, she spun the cylinder as she headed for the door, making sure a live cartridge would line up next under the firing pin. She froze in mid-step.

There were only four live rounds left.

This morning before Mason left the house there were five, now that he was back, only four. Obviously, he'd taken it with him and fired it again. Whom had he shot now?

She pondered this a moment and was rewarded with a sure and clear answer. The knowledge that he had likely murdered again canceled any last doubts she'd had about her plan. For once in her life she was taking charge, making a tough decision, acting with forethought, unbridled by the possibility of dire consequence or judgment error. This was it. There was no turning back.

She walked the length of the hallway back toward Mason's room like it was the proverbial tunnel of white light. She was beyond fear, beyond sorrow. This was doing what must be done. She could stand no more stress. If it was she who died today, so be it. There must at least be relief in that.

She strode quietly back through Mason's open door with the gun hanging passively at her side. He paid her no attention, probably never noticed she was gone. Now in a sitting position on the edge of the bed, he was poring over a three-ring binder of equipment procedure, still trying to decipher the blank tapes.

Monica moved to the roll-top and lifted a multi-page document from beneath a pile of papers that looked like they hadn't been moved for months.

"Mason, I know why the tapes are blank."

"Is that so?" he said without looking up. "And why is that?"

"Because in the middle of the night I threw the circuit breaker to your room."

He looked up now, studying her for several seconds before seeing the gun at her side. He didn't seem to panic right away, even after spotting it.

"Why would you do that?"

"Because I guessed correctly, with hints from you, that you were ignoring your data in favor of Paul's, and that you would miss the recording lapse. I wanted to put you in a position of equality with me."

"What is this?" he asked.

"I came to your room last night with this gun in my hand, prepared to kill you for no other reason than self-preservation, only to find that you'd installed a deadbolt lock to protect yourself from the unknown after nine p.m. That's when I decided I had to surprise you another way and hatched this scheme."

"What are you going to do with that?" He pointed at the gun.

"I have to kill you, Mason."

"It's Paul, isn't it?" he said, swallowing hard. "I suspected you two. You make a foolish mistake choosing him over me, but in either case, this isn't necessary." He gestured at the gun. "You're not married. Take the man and go. Chase your juvenile dreams."

"Don't patronize me, Mason. I know he's dead. You shot him."

"Ridiculous."

"This gun only has four bullets now. This morning there were five, and the morning before, when you took it to Atlantic City, there were six. One was for Paul. Who got the other one, Roger Wilkins?" She waved the gun as she referred to it, still not aiming it at him.

His expression began to melt down. Still he played coy.

"You're mad."

She raised the gun and pointed it in his general direction. "Did you kill Wilkins too, Mason?"

He thought for a minute before answering. "I had to."

Now it made sense. "Covering your tracks, huh? I'm next, right?"

"Monica, you don't know what you're saying. Whatever I did, I did for us."

"Too bad you didn't consult me first."

"So you've named yourself judge and jury."

"Look at what your research has done to you, Mason. You're crazy. We both know there's only one person alive now who can stop you."

"I always placed you above cheap romance, Monica. Paul Fontana was hardly worthy of your affections, and your revenge is not worth the price you'll pay."

"He was far more worthy than you. Nevertheless, I might agree if revenge were my sole motive here, Mason, but as it is, I took the liberty of drafting this revised will on your computer while you were out this morning." She held up the freshly printed document.

He stared at her now with his mouth hanging open. The full impact of what he was in for sank in.

"That's right, Mason. I found the voided version. That's not fair after all I've done for you. I located the file for the original will in the computer and made a minor change, bequeathing a modest sum to the university, with the rest, of course, still going to me. There's a note in here, too, to the lawyer explaining the change and the voided original." She stepped forward and set it on the bed near him. From the desk behind her and to the left she tossed him a pen.

"After what you've done to me I deserve the money, Mason. Sign the will and the letter to the lawyer. Date them both today."

He was still thinking optimistically. "I could just change it later."

"You won't have the chance."

He went pale. "You'll never get away with this."

"Maybe not, but it'll take one heck of a detective to make anything more of this than suicide after I wipe the gun clean and place it in your hand. It's pretty cut and dried. A jealous man kills, then kills again to hide it, and then finds he can't live with himself and takes his own life too. It's a classic murder-suicide."

She studied him closely. It was as if time had slowed to half-speed and she could clearly see everything in minute detail. Mason still sat on the bed. The binder lay open in his lap and his arms hung limp at his side with the shoulders slouched. His fingers shook uncontrollably. Facing death is an unpleasant experience, she thought, but this must be especially hard for Mason, knowing he was about to die without seeing it beforehand and having the opportunity to divert it as he was accustomed. How he must feel to suddenly realize he's a mere mortal after all, must be quite a shock, the ultimate cure for god-complex.

She looked at her hand, dangling in space before her, loosely holding the weapon. She was struck by how steady it was. This wasn't how she expected it to go. Her plan was good, but the weak spot, she knew, was herself. Could she stand and aim a gun at another person? Could she really pull the trigger? That was unknown. At the very least, she expected great volumes of tears and much shaking, but she was remarkably calm. Her plan was successful and she was in absolute control. She could now imagine how Mason must have felt with the power he wielded. Whatever the goal and whatever the outcome, managing one's own destiny was a good feeling.

Mason began to whimper. His lower jaw quivered, and tears formed in his eyes. "Monica, don't do this, please. I'll give you anything you want. I always have. You know that."

It was a pitiful display, the venerable Mason Brooks, Ph.D., professor, author, now reduced to tears and begging for mercy. His pleas touched her, but there in her heart, too, was the rage over two years of abuse and manipulation at his hands, the hands

of a murderer who would surely kill her if she didn't kill him
first. A man who if left unchecked could wreak untold horror
upon an unsuspecting world. For a moment she saw her father sitting there on the bed whimpering, pleading, apologizing. Mason
embodied all that was wrong in her life, all the mistakes she had
made, and all the fears she would no longer run from. Her life
would never be the same. Never again would inaction and self-
doubt cripple her.

She firmed her grip on the Smith and Wesson, stepped forward,
and took aim at his forehead.

"Sign the will, Mason."

He picked up the pen and paper. Scanning the letter and will,
he shook his head and muttered to himself. Pen in hand, he
moved to sign the two documents, but vacillated and eventually
stopped and put the pen back down at his side.

"I won't do it, Monica. I won't give you the satisfaction. You'll
shoot me either way, so I haven't anything to lose by not signing
this."

"I considered the possibility that you'd refuse. Remember that
when you're dead, you're dead, so what 'you' have is nothing to
gain. Whether I have your money won't matter to you then, and
I beg to differ. You do have something to lose."

She stepped closer yet and slowly lowered her aim from his
forehead to his crotch.

"Don't be a fool, Mason. There are four bullets in this gun. I
only need one to kill you. The other three could make this a very
long and painful ordeal."

He flinched at the thought.

"Sign it," she said forcefully.

"You'd never do it."

She cocked the hammer with her thumb and inched the gun
closer to his groin.

Without hesitation Mason picked up the pen and signed both
the will and letter.

"Slide them over," Monica said, pointing with her free, left hand toward the end of the bed.

Mason did as she ordered.

Carefully reaching in, she snatched the papers and set them aside.

"Now, swing your legs up onto the bed and lie back."

"Monica, please—"

"Do it!" she screamed at him.

Reluctantly, he did.

"Close your eyes."

He closed them, but as he did, he mustered as much calm in his voice as possible and made one last desperate plea for mercy.

"Monica, you can't do this. Think of the research. Think about what this means to the world. My discovery is bigger than you and me and our insignificant troubles. If I die, the world may never know and humanity may never benefit from all we've done."

"Yes," she said, "I almost forgot. The research, that's the fascinating part of all this. You know, you were right all along."

"About what?"

"About the bond. 'Love is a bond stronger than life itself.'"

"What are you talking about?"

"Don't you recognize it, Mason? It's the inscription on Paul's bracelet, the one from his dying mother."

She raised her left arm vertically so the loose sleeve of her blouse slipped down to her elbow, revealing the bracelet Paul had left with her before going to Atlantic City.

"Look, Mason."

He opened his eyes and saw the bracelet. First he had a look of recognition, then comprehension. His eyes flashed with terror, then slowly, he settled back into the bed and seemed to accept what had always been inevitable.

"That's right, Mason, it never was Paul. The bracelet was always there in your dreams. You just never saw it, or thought to look for it. Apparently the bond is more difficult to break than you ever imagined, and fate can't be fooled."

She released the catch, removed the bracelet from her wrist, and tossed it onto Mason's chest. "Here, you hold onto this for a while. Make it official."

Mason Brooks gripped the bracelet with one hand and closed his eyes again, this time of his own volition.

Monica stepped in close, held the revolver to his left temple, and...couldn't pull the trigger.

Suddenly vengeance and money meant nothing. She knew now how deeply she loved Paul, but she simply couldn't kill in cold blood, not for Paul's sake or her own. It wouldn't bring Paul back. She recalled her own revulsion at the thought of Paul killing Mason for the same motives. Why should she be different? This was fate's job, not hers.

There was no fear, only pity and sorrow. She was tired, very, very tired. All she wanted was to quit and leave.

Maybe it was time to go home.

Mason reacted instantly to the hesitation. His left hand shot up from his side and grabbed Monica's wrist. He fully extended his arm past his head, dragging the gun hand with it. The sudden movement caused the weapon to discharge, the bullet narrowly missing his head as the barrel moved upward.

Mason rolled off the bed and onto his feet in one swift motion. He twisted Monica's gun hand violently, throwing her off balance, and swung his right elbow around and drove it into her side. She buckled at the waist and crashed sideways into a stack of electronic equipment. The .38 fell from her hand, bounced off the bed and dropped to the floor. Monica fell too, landing on her side on the hardwood floor, three feet from the gun.

She lunged desperately for the gun, hoping to keep it from Mason's hand. Mason stomped down hard with a composite-soled shoe and pinned her left hand to the floor, her fingers only inches from the gun. There was a crunching sound when he stomped, and searing pain shot up her arm.

She screamed.

Still pinning her hand, Mason stooped and retrieved the

weapon. With the gun aimed at her face, he finally released her hand.

"You should have acted while you had the chance, dearie. You always were indecisive. You'll come to regret this lost opportunity."

Monica sat up and tended to her hand. The pain was nearly unbearable. At least two fingers were clearly broken.

"I already do. You'd better shoot me while you can, Mason. I won't make the same mistake twice."

"Oh, I plan on it, my dear Monica, but first I have something in mind. Get up." He motioned with the gun for her to rise.

It took some effort for her to stand. Her side ached and she cradled the damaged hand with her good one.

"Sit on the bed," he said.

She was nearly faint, and her sitting was as much coincidence as compliance.

Mason kneaded the bracelet he still held in one hand. He tossed it up and down a few times and then read the inscription.

"I'll have to admit, you had me going there for a minute. You're clever, Monica. I underestimated you, I see. I never seriously considered an inanimate object as the source. It even sounds plausible. Too bad you were wrong."

With a smile and a shake of his head, he tossed the bracelet aside and it slid across the floor.

"Now," he said, turning his attention and the gun again to Monica, "remove your clothing."

Monica's heart stopped. "Don't even think it."

"Oh, yes. Unfinished business. One last little dance."

"I won't do it."

Mason leveled the gun at her eyes and a rage ignited across his face. She had never seen such a red-faced look of pure evil.

He screamed at her so hard that spit flew from his mouth and the gun wavered dangerously. "Strip, damn you, or so help me I'll tear the clothes off you myself."

Chapter 30

Paul's greatest threat came not from the police, but from falling asleep at the wheel. He'd heard that one symptom of head concussions is drowsiness, and whether that was the cause, or it was the drugs or the poor night's 'sleep' he'd had beneath the pier, he could barely keep his eyes open.

Even at ninety to one hundred miles per hour, a speed sure to keep most weary travelers wide-eyed, he continually nodded. He tried everything, blasting the radio, freezing with the window open, and talking to himself out loud. Nothing helped for long. Fifty miles from home he fell asleep long enough for the ambulance to drift off the fast lane and sideswipe the guardrail in a loud and spectacular display of grinding metal. That kept him awake for a while. No doubt it did the same for the drivers near him too.

In the end, it was sheer anger and force of will that kept his eyes peeled open and the vehicle on the road.

The ambulance was an irritation. Surprisingly gutless and unresponsive, he wished for the Corvette. Of course, at this speed the Corvette would have attracted every highway patrol car in five counties.

Even with the ambulance, as he exited the freeway and pulled into town, he was shocked to have made it the whole way without being stopped. He'd expected a roadblock, or at least a fleet of squad cars and a squadron of helicopters to converge on him.

Now he wasn't sure it would do him much good to have made it through, as tired as he was. How ridiculous it would look as he tried to save Monica with a big yawn on his face. He pictured himself as the cowardly lion in the Wizard of Oz, falling asleep in the poppy field on the doorstep of Emerald City.

Unlike the lion, though, there was no good witch watching over him. As he passed through uptown, lights and siren still blaring, he tried not to focus on the fact that the deja vu he was counting on to direct his actions wasn't happening. It was beginning to look like a guts and glory operation. Against Mason, it wasn't likely to be pretty.

A few blocks from Brooks' home, he doused the lights and siren. It seemed like the right thing to do, but, ironically, Mason probably knew he was coming just as surely as if he'd arrived with a brass band.

Just as he'd done only days earlier, Paul eased slowly to the curb in front of Mason's row house and killed the engine. Looking over the house, he saw nothing unusual, nothing indicating a threat. He pressed on.

Once out of the ambulance, he shut the door quietly and moved toward the front door with his eyes on the windows. Nothing there.

Whatever drugs they had given him at the hospital had now worn off. The pain in his head returned with a vengeance. His stomach was unstable too, but the bleeding from his arm had stopped for now, and suddenly he was having no trouble staying awake.

Climbing the steps to the door, he turned the handle ever so slowly. It was locked. That figures.

Stepping back on the stoop, he scanned the facade, looking for another entry point. Wrought-iron bars covered all the windows. The ivy would definitely not support his weight if he were to try climbing to the roof, and what would he do if he got there? Since this was a row house, he'd have to run around the block to the alley to reach any back entrance. Gaining easy entry there was probably no more likely. He'd have to kick the front door in.

That wouldn't work either, he quickly realized, recalling the paper booties covering his bare feet. There wasn't time for this. He had to get Monica. Stepping back down two steps, he charged the solid door and threw his shoulder and all his weight into it.

It didn't budge.

A car came down the street. Paul tried to act as if he were ringing the doorbell while it passed. That gave him time to appreciate his impact with the door. His head felt like a pumpkin in the hands of a juvenile delinquent on Halloween night. His shoulder was more numb than pained. Which was worrisome. And, naturally, his arm was bleeding again.

Oddly, the loud bang brought no one to the door. Perhaps they weren't home. He hadn't come this far to turn away, though. Sure that he'd at least heard some cracking and may have weakened the doorjamb, he gave himself a bit more room than the first attempt and again took a run at the door.

There was definite cracking this time, either the door or his ribs, maybe both, but again the door held fast. He never realized pain could get this bad.

Looking around the neighborhood, it didn't appear that he'd attracted attention yet, but this couldn't go on. This time he coolly retraced his steps all the way down the walk to the ambulance before turning and sprinting full speed at the door. He launched himself and, like a karate master breaking a stack of bricks, committed every fiber to the effort.

The door blasted open and Paul sprawled headlong into the foyer, skidding on the tile floor amid bits of broken wood trim. He might have blacked out momentarily, but in the panic and pain couldn't be sure even of that.

On the drive up, he'd imagined himself easing the door open with no squeaks and peeking in like a SWAT team member on assignment, sliding inside and getting against the foyer wall undetected. So much for plans.

His vision wasn't clear anymore. Exhausted by the ordeal with the door and weakened by lack of food, he struggled to his feet and wavered there, off balance. Hell of a time to think pizza.

He shuffled along the wall and glanced into the den.

No one was there.

Was he wrong? Had Mason not returned? Doubts started to creep in. The fog was settling again. Had he stolen the ambulance and driven all the way here for nothing?

Suddenly the silence was broken by a scream from upstairs, explaining why his noisy entrance went unnoticed. It was a woman's voice. Monica!

Paul lunged forward...and stopped.

It's a trap. Mason knew he was coming, knew it all day. He set the snare. Monica's the bait. If you go up those stairs, you'll die.

Monica screamed again, a horrific scream. Paul couldn't turn away from it. There was no going back now, trap or no trap. She needed his help. He'd been right about that. Maybe he'd been right about everything else too.

Trust your instincts.

He bounded up the stairs, three steps at a time. Halfway up he should have cut it back to two steps. He caught his toe and his wobbly legs deflated. Falling forward, he sprawled painfully on the stairs like a bug on a windshield, his knees, shins and chin taking the brunt especially hard.

Gathering himself, he rose and finished the climb. At the top he paused long enough to figure out which direction the sounds were coming from. To his left toward Mason's lab at the hall's end he heard angry words. Mason was shouting at her.

That seemed odd. What sort of trap was this?

The lab door was mostly closed, but not latched. Paul made a decision as he raced toward it. Peeking through it didn't 'feel' right. He blasted through the door, giving it everything he had, this time with his uninjured shoulder. We're getting good at this now. The door swung open so hard that it bent back the spring-style doorstop and the inside door handle punched through the sheetrock and held the door fast in the wide-open position.

Monica lay on her back on the bed. She was stripped half-naked and her clothes were in tatters. Her nose was bleeding and contusions surrounded her cheekbones. She was putting up quite a struggle.

Mason kneeled over her on the bed, twisting her arm with one hand and wielding the revolver in the other.

"Monica!" Paul shouted at the sight of her lying there, damaged and prone. He stood just inside the doorway, feet apart, braced for recovery from the collision with the door and as defense against the unknown.

Paul's shout was punctuation to the explosion of the door.

Mason pivoted at the hips, and total disbelief covered his face at the sight of Paul Fontana standing in his home, a living ghost.

Paul looked into the crazed eyes of Mason Brooks and saw that, somehow, his arrival had been a complete surprise.

"You?" he said. "How did you—"

"Get out, Paul!" Monica screamed.

Mason returned his attention to Monica long enough to pistol-whip her across the forehead to silence her in his moment of confusion.

Paul didn't hesitate. He charged the bed, a primal groan forcing its way up his throat.

Mason spun his gun hand in the direction of the charging intruder and fired one shot.

The bullet caught Paul in the fleshy upper thigh, ripping clean through the leg and ricocheting into a far wall. The impact lifted his leg and threw it back, twirling Paul and hurling him against the wall in a heap.

Stunned but conscious, Paul lay motionless for a moment, awaiting the second and final shot. When it didn't come, he cracked an eye and spied Mason again preoccupied with Monica, seemingly intent on finishing what he'd started with her.

Surprisingly, she was still conscious. Lying beneath Mason, she stared at him with a look of pure hatred, eyes flashing, teeth bared. There was a toughness there, a quality and depth neither man previously knew existed.

Paul loved her now more than ever.

His leg felt odd, but there was no pain. He was losing too much blood, and at some level knew time was critical if he were to act. Shock or blood-loss would incapacitate him shortly.

He quietly propped himself up on one arm and leaned back against the wall. It was all too clear what Mason was up to with Monica, and it would be torture to witness it. His leg didn't respond to instructions. Panic set in.

Mason caught Paul's movement out of the corner of his eye and again swung the gun in his direction. "Are you still alive?" he said. "You're a tough bastard to kill." He took careful aim at Paul's face and started to squeeze the trigger.

Paul sat helpless against the wall.

Mason pulled up before firing, though. "Wait," he said. "Get up."

Soaked in his own blood, Paul made a feeble and futile attempt. "I can't," he said.

Mason smiled cruelly. "Just as I thought. I'll take care of you in a minute. First, there's something I'd like you to watch. You'll get a kick out of this."

Mason resumed his assault on Monica, now deriving bonus pleasure with his two-for-one torture scheme.

Over my dead body, Paul thought. With his good arm as a crutch, he tried to lift himself onto his good knee. He would crawl to Monica if he had to.

As he adjusted the position of his hand on the floor along the base of the wall, he felt an object. Looking down at it, he recognized it as his bracelet. What was it doing there?

Love is a bond stronger than life itself....

Paul clasped the bracelet in his hand and shouted Mason's name with urgency.

Again surprised to hear the voice of the pesky and seemingly immortal Paul Fontana, Mason diverted his attention once more from Monica to Paul.

The gun hand came swinging out too. Maybe his minute was up.

Timing his move, Paul leaned off the support of his good hand and launched the bracelet sidearm, aiming directly for Mason's face. Then he allowed himself to fall horizontally in the hope that it would make him a more difficult target.

As Mason came around, a flying object approaching his face was the first thing he saw. Instinctively, he threw his head off to one side and closed his eyes. He released Monica's arm and brought his left hand up to deflect the unknown projectile.

Like a well-placed horseshoe toss, the spinning bracelet caught one of Mason's splayed fingers and hung on, a perfect ringer.

Mason looked with horror at the persistent bracelet dangling from his hand, a black magic trinket, an omen of personal doom.

Monica didn't waste the opportunity with Mason distracted and her arm free. With all her might, she kicked upward and sank her knee into Mason's crotch as he straddled her on the bed. When he jackknifed forward on reflex, she followed the kick with a massive right cross to the jaw.

Mason's head flew out to the side, and he teetered over the edge of the bed, flailing his arms to regain balance.

Monica didn't let him get the chance. Again her knee sank home.

Mason toppled off the bed to his side with arms peddling air, tangling himself in various electrical cords draped between the equipment and the bed. Gyrating like an aged gymnast in a failed maneuver, he landed hard, face down. His left arm remained in the air, caught in the cords, bent back in an awkward and painful-looking position. His gun hand tried to cushion the fall, but with the fingers wrapped around the gun, it only curled up under his belly.

As his torso hit the ground, there was a muffled yet loud report. The gun had fired.

Mason lay still.

Paul and Monica froze in disbelief. Monica moved first, easing off the bed and nudging Mason with a toe, softly at first, and then outright kicking him hard in the side. He didn't move. Kneeling down, she rolled him over far enough to see a pool of blood beneath him. She checked for a pulse. There was none.

She stood and looked at Paul. "He's dead," she said with surprise. Still dangling in the air next to her was Mason's arm. She removed the bracelet from his fingers and looked at it with awe, then rushed to Paul's side.

Kneeling down, holding her crushed hand out and away, she hugged him vigorously, causing him great pain.

"I'm sorry," she said, hearing him moan.

"That's okay. It hurts so good."

"I thought you were dead."

"So did I."

"What happened to your head?"

"I stopped for a haircut. It's the newest style. Extreme barbering."

"What's with the doctor's getup?"

"I thought you might need some medical assistance."

She smiled at him with tears in her eyes. "You're the one who needs a doctor. We've got to get you an ambulance."

"Don't bother. I brought my own. It's parked out front."

"You silly fool," she said, touching his lips.

"I don't think we should say anything about Mason's discovery to anyone, not even the police," Paul said, wincing from his various wounds. "He said he hadn't written anything down. The secret can die with us. The world isn't ready for it."

"How do we explain all this then?" she motioned toward Mason's body.

"Like that would be an explanation?"

She nodded. Studying the bracelet in her hand again, she placed it in Paul's. "I think you'd better keep this."

Not understanding, Paul was hurt by the gesture.

"I prefer rings, myself," she said.

Paul smiled as her meaning sank in.

"There wouldn't be much of a life with me," he said. "I've got nothing, not even a job. With Mason gone, now I'll never learn to get rich."

Monica peered over at some papers lying on the desk and shrugged.

"Don't worry," she said. "I think we have all we need."

LOOK FOR THESE
SALVO PRESS BOOKS

FATAL NETWORK
Trevor Scott   0-9664520-0-3, $12.95

ENEMY WITHIN
Phillip Thompson   0-9664520-2-X, $11.00

MEMPHIS RIBS
Gerald Duff   0-9664520-1-1, $12.95

EXTREME FACTION
Trevor Scott   0-9664520-3-8, $12.95

THE SACRED DISC
Charles West   0-9664520-4-6, $12.95

WAKE UP DEAD
Christopher Bonn Jonnes   0-9664520-5-4, $12.95

HOUDINI AND THE SEANCE MURDERS
Christopher Farran   0-9664520-6-2, $12.95

CODEBREAKER
Katherine Myers   0-9664520-9-7, $16.95

THE DOLOMITE SOLUTION
Trevor Scott   0-9664520-7-0, $12.95

SNAKE SONG
Gerald Duff   0-9664520-8-9, $12.95

Available at your local bookstore and most online stores.
Read more about these and other titles online at:
www.salvopress.com